First Love

Kisses

First Love

by Diane Namm

WESTWIND

Troll Associates

For Richard—my first love

Chapter One

*T*he wind blew through Amanda Townsend's ash-blonde hair as she drove her new white Mustang convertible down the street. Amanda glanced in the rearview mirror to check out her outfit. She loved the way the small-sized white T-shirt and fitted black lace vest went with her jeans. Her friends at school all envied the way she dressed, always putting together great outfits out of different pieces.

Amanda wrinkled her nose, remembering her mother's comments that morning. "Really, Amanda, is that any way to dress for work?"

"Mother, it's *my* job, and I'll dress however I want," Amanda had replied tartly. Then she had slammed out of the house, leaving her mother calling after her.

Shaking her head to rid herself of this morning's all-too-familiar battle of wills, Amanda focused back on the street signs. Afraid she had missed the KSS-TV station while she'd been thinking about her mother, Amanda slowed down to check the street addresses. Her car drifted slowly over to the left.

Amanda didn't see Hero Montoya on his rebuilt '66 FLH Harley-Davidson coming up behind her until someone on the sidewalk shouted, "Look out!"

The Harley roared to a stop just in time. Amanda's brakes squealed.

"Nice driving. Where'd you get your license, from a mail-order catalog?" Hero growled, taking off his helmet and shaking out his thick brown hair.

But when he saw Amanda, Hero's face flushed, deepening his smoothly tanned skin against his bright white T-shirt.

Hero Montoya had moved to Cliffside in the middle of last semester. He'd entered Cliffside High two thirds of the way through sophomore year, and he hadn't had a chance to make any real friends. A loner by nature, Hero usually stood on the fringes of every crowd, never really connecting with anyone, but noticing everything that went on around him. And he had definitely noticed Amanda Townsend.

Everyone knew Amanda Townsend, the most beautiful girl in Cliffside High. Amanda was at the center of every crowd, especially the jock set. Her large violet eyes always sparkled, especially when she laughed. Hero wondered what it would be like to be the one who made her laugh and have her turn the full light of her eyes on him.

Hero had never expected Amanda to notice him at school. After all, why would the most popular girl in school bother with the new guy in town, especially when he lived on the wrong side of it? Now he'd just had his big chance, and, instead of playing it up, he'd practically bitten off her head. Hero wanted to kick himself.

Amanda blushed furiously, looking contrite.

"I'm so sorry," Amanda said. "I was just checking the address, and I looked down for a second, and I wasn't expecting anyone behind me, and . . ." Her voice trailed off as she looked into Hero's dark brown eyes.

Amanda noticed immediately how incredibly handsome Hero was: his thick brown hair, the broad shoulders and arms that neatly filled out his white T-shirt, which was tucked into his well-worn jeans.

Then Amanda spotted the Cliffside High parking sticker on his motorcycle.

How come I never noticed this guy before? Amanda thought to herself. Then she remembered her best friend, Samantha

Walker, babbling about some cute new guy who lived on the wrong side of Cliffside Drive and rode a motorcycle to school every day.

Samantha was right about one thing. This guy was definitely cute.

"Are you hurt?" Amanda asked with concern. Leave it to me to make someone feel right at home, she thought disgustedly.

"Hey, no, I'm all right," Hero answered hastily, running his hand through the front lock of his hair, which was always falling down over his forehead. "I shouldn't have tried to pass you. It's just I was in a real hurry to get to my new job," Hero said.

Before Amanda could reply, Keera Johnson, a slim, brown-haired girl wearing neat jeans and a light green tank top, ran up to where Hero and Amanda had almost collided.

"Are you guys okay?" she asked.

"I'm a little shaken up," Amanda admitted. "How about you?" she asked, turning to Hero.

"I'm fine," Hero assured them both. He didn't want Amanda to think he was a whiner.

"Thanks for calling out to me. It was you, wasn't it?" Amanda asked the girl.

Shyly, Keera nodded.

"I was so afraid that I'd miss the address for the KSS-TV cable station and be late for my first day at work, I guess I stopped watching the road," Amanda began.

Hero and Keera each stared at Amanda as if she had two heads.

Seeing their faces, Amanda started to say, "I know it was stupid, but . . ."

"I was headed for KSS-TV, too," Hero said in amazement. He couldn't believe his good luck.

"You're working at KSS?" Keera asked in disbelief. It never occurred to her that she and someone like Amanda Townsend would ever have any interest in common. And Amanda couldn't possibly need the money.

Like Hero, Keera Johnson also knew Amanda Townsend from Cliffside High. Who didn't? It was impossible not to notice Amanda in her cool clothes—surrounded by guys, the envy of most of the girls. Totally unapproachable, Keera had thought until this moment.

"Smashing start, huh?" Amanda said, smiling faintly.

Amanda parked her car in front of the station, and Hero pulled his motorcycle into the space behind her. All three walked up the uneven path to the trailer door that was labeled in tiny, hard-to-read letters "KSS-TV." The door was locked.

"Good thing we were all in a hurry," Hero commented drily.

Amanda flushed, still feeling guilty about almost running over Hero.

Way to go, Hero said grimly to himself, seeing Amanda's reaction. Trying to figure some way out of his personally engraved black hole, Hero shifted uneasily from one leg to another.

Just then tall, lanky Jamar Williams rode up the narrow path almost to the doorway of the cable station on his bike, leg muscles pumping, headset plugged in, and in some other world. His loose-fitting muscle shirt flapped around the knotted muscles in his hard stomach as he careened to a halt a few feet away from where Hero, Amanda, and Keera were standing.

Tying his bike to a nearby tree trunk, Jamar, still oblivious to everything but the music in his head, looked up and saw Keera. He stopped in the middle of what he was doing and pulled off his multicolored bandanna, disconnecting his headset at the same time.

"Hey! I know you. You're Keera Johnson, the genius," Jamar said, smiling at her warmly.

Keera blushed furiously.

"That's right, I knew you looked familiar," Amanda said. "You're the one who's always winning those science awards!"

Keera didn't know what to say. She couldn't believe that Amanda Townsend—or anyone other than her friends at school—would know who she was.

"Do you know this guy?" Hero asked.

"Be cool, Keera! I won't bite, promise. The name's Jamar Williams, Jam to my friends."

"I'm Amanda Townsend," Amanda said cheerfully, taking up the introductions. She liked Jamar immediately, and no one could resist his wide open smile and the way his eyes crinkled when he spoke.

Turning to Hero, Amanda said with a laugh, "I almost ran you over, but I don't even know your name."

"Hero Montoya," Hero said with a slight grin, holding his hand out to Jamar.

"Nice to meet you, Hero," Jamar answered. Then he pointed to the motorcycle parked behind Amanda's car.

"Is that your old pile of reject Harley parts?" Jamar asked.

Hero's eyes flared at the insult. But before he could reply, Jamar added hastily, "Lighten up, dude, I'm playing with you." Jamar laughed and slapped Hero's hand.

It was contagious. Keera and Amanda got the giggles, and Hero cracked a rare smile. Amanda noticed that Hero looked very nice when he smiled.

"So, are you working at KSS, too?" Hero asked.

"Absolutely. For the entire summer. My guidance counselor, Mr. Fredericks, told me I'm supposed to see a Mr. Drew Pearson, station manager of KSS-TV," Jamar said.

"You're going to be working at the cable station?" Keera asked. I can't believe this guy wants to work in television, she thought to herself.

"Definitely," Jamar replied. "It's the best way to start building my band's rep."

"Mr. Fredericks got me the job here, too," Amanda spoke up enthusiastically. "I told him how tired I was of just hanging around at the Yacht Club, doing the same old thing summer after summer, and he suggested I work with Mr. Pearson, too. Isn't that a coincidence?"

At the mention of the Yacht Club, Hero rolled his eyes. He should have known Amanda was a rich kid.

Amanda saw Hero's look and immediately iced up. Turning away from Hero, she asked Keera, "Did Mr. Fredericks send you here, too?"

"I answered the notice on the school job board," Keera replied shyly.

"Me, too," Hero added.

"Do any of you know what working at a television station's supposed to be like?" Amanda asked. "I'm really excited about it, but I haven't a clue what we're supposed to be doing."

"Well, music's my thing. And my band—we're hoping for a little local exposure, recording some videos, expanding our horizons, the whole deal. Maybe you've heard of us, JellyJam?" Jamar asked hopefully.

Amanda shook her head. Keera and Hero looked clueless.

"Well, after a few appearances on local cable, my friend Rogue thinks we'll be in demand all over Cliffside—and then who knows where we'll go after that," Jamar said with confidence.

Amanda smiled her fabulous smile at Jamar, and Jamar smiled back. He's cute, Amanda thought to herself. This job is definitely going to be interesting.

Then Jamar turned to Keera and grinned. Keera had caught Jamar's eye at school, but he'd been so busy writing and rehearsing new music for the band that he hadn't had a chance to approach her. But just last week, his best friend and the lead singer of his band, Rogue Jelsen, had told Jamar who Keera was.

Jamar, who usually had his eyes on the keyboard and not on girls, hadn't dated much. But when he looked at Keera, he liked what he saw. Jamar had wanted to talk to her before school ended, but Rogue had told Jamar to forget her—she hung around with the library geeks, and she wasn't going to be messing around with someone like Jamar.

But seeing Keera here before him, Jamar was willing to take his chances. He could care less who she hung out with. Besides, it must have been fate that they ended up in the same summer job. Keera was the sweetest thing he'd ever seen. Summer was beginning to look long and happy.

"So, Hero, what's your story?" Amanda said with a slight challenge in her voice, remembering Hero's scornful look.

Looking straight at Amanda, Hero replied evenly, "I need the job, and working at a cable station sounded more fun than busing tables. Yacht club slumming wasn't an option for me," Hero couldn't help adding.

Two angry spots of color appeared on Amanda's cheeks. This guy is a jerk, she thought.

Hero winced. What is wrong with me

today? he asked himself. Usually he could talk his way through any situation. He knew how to be charming. But, somehow, being this close to Amanda made him act like a total dork.

Before Amanda could come up with a snappy retort, everyone turned at the sound of screeching tires and a scratchy clutch. A battered, forest green Saab pulled up halfway onto the curb. A tall, handsome man practically spilled out of the car, juggling files, tapes, and newspapers, and fumbling for his keys.

"Hey, guys, sorry I'm late. Drew Pearson, station manager." Drew held out his hand to shake, then looked down at the things in his arms and shrugged, nearly dropping everything in the process.

"Here, let me help you with that," Amanda offered, attempting to hold some of Drew's stuff while he unlocked the door.

"Okay, thanks—uh, Amanda, isn't it?" Drew said.

"That's right, Mr. Pearson," Amanda said, giving Drew her most dazzling smile.

Now this guy is really good-looking, Amanda thought. She was flattered that he knew her name and that he didn't call her "Ms. Townsend" in that awful formal way her teachers always did.

Jamar and Keera looked at Drew, then at each other. Drew wasn't exactly what either of them had expected, but then again, who was? To break up the awkward silence while everyone waited for Drew to open the door, Jamar did a moonwalk behind Drew's back. Keera covered her giggle with a cough.

Standing close enough to smell Drew's musky cologne and to count the threads on the blue cotton shirt that perfectly matched his clear blue eyes, Amanda felt her heart start to race. Hero's last insult flew out of her mind. Who cared what someone like Hero thought when Drew was around?

Amanda gazed frankly at Drew, comparing him to the men and boys she knew at Cliffside High. The teachers were ancient and most of them smelled a little like formaldehyde. And the guys were gawky and awkward—high school boys just seemed hopelessly clueless.

Amanda shuddered as she remembered Samantha telling her about her latest grope. Samantha giggled like a fool and thought it was funny, but Amanda didn't want some grubby guy slobbering over her.

Of course, there was always Tyler Scott, who had been her friend since they could toddle. Amanda's parents loved Tyler, and their families had been friends forever. But Amanda couldn't imagine kissing Tyler. After all, they used to play jump rope together!

But Drew was a grown-up, and a very good-looking one, too.

"Thanks for the help, Amanda." Drew flashed Amanda a grin, breaking into her train of thought.

Amanda smiled back brightly.

"By the way," Drew added, leading the four of them into the darkened station office, flipping on lights as he walked. "I'm not Mr. Pearson. Mr. Pearson's my father, a stodgy old rich banker who can't figure out what I'm doing in television. Just call me Drew."

Drew gave Amanda the desk closest to his office and assigned the other three desks in the room to Hero, Keera, and Jamar.

Amanda was delighted. She'd be able to watch Drew through the glass walls of his office. That would definitely help to take her mind off that irritating Hero.

"How about I give you folks the tour?" Drew asked. Without waiting for an answer, he started to walk through the station, speaking quickly as he walked.

"You're probably wondering why you're all here and what you'll be doing. Well, I got this vision of student programming by and for the kids in Cliffside, and I convinced some of the corporate-powers-that-be in this town to support it. So, here you guys are. Now it's up to you to decide what we're going to do."

Pointing to a windowless room with bright track spotlights and free-standing lamps, Drew informed them that this was the studio where all in-house taping was usually done. Behind a glass panel were microphones and sound equipment, where music could be recorded, mixed, and taped live or added later to any program.

Jamar was especially interested in the music controls. "I'm there," Jamar nodded with certainty, making a mental note to check out that panel later on.

Amanda was a little awed by all the serious-looking taping equipment.

Catching Amanda's expression, Drew laughed and gently touched her shoulder. "It looks a lot more complicated than it is," Drew explained. "Don't worry, I'll be able to show you everything you need to know. In a couple of days, you'll be a pro."

Amanda was doubtful, especially as they walked into the control room, which contained about thirty television monitors and screens.

"This is where you'll mix your footage—location and studio shots—and decide which camera angles to use, how much footage from each camera, stuff like that. Then you'll put together your whole show," Drew said. "To begin with, each of you will put together a fifteen-minute segment, so that we'll have an hour-long special. If it flies, we'll discuss whether to keep the show as a special or make it weekly."

Amanda groaned in dismay. This was beginning to sound a lot like real work, and she didn't think she was ever going to be able to figure out how to deal with all these machines.

Despite Drew's enthusiasm and the state-of-the-art technology, Amanda couldn't help noticing the low ceiling, the cracked flooring, the worn carpeting, and the unflattering fluorescent lighting that flickered on and off, making the station seem like it was stuck in a time warp where no sunlight ever shone.

For a moment the luxurious lawns, shiny white docks, and colorful sailboats silhouetted against the bright blue summer sky at the Yacht Club beckoned. Then Amanda remembered her mother's reaction when she had told her about her plans for the summer.

"Really, Amanda—a job? You're not even responsible enough to keep your room straightened up on Consuela's day off, and you still haven't figured out how to use the computer you wanted so badly for Christmas. How are you ever going to work all the complicated machinery at a television station? And why would you even want to bother when you could be sailing or playing tennis at the Club?" her mother had asked critically.

Amanda was determined to prove her mother wrong. She wasn't going to spend another stifling summer at the Club with her mother's friends and the usual crowd.

Instead she was going to learn everything there was to working at KSS-TV. Who knows—maybe she'd even become a reporter some day, and she'd do an in-depth special on famous daughters who became successful in spite of their critical, snobby mothers!

Looking directly at Drew, his face brimming with confidence and enthusiasm, Amanda caught her breath. He's so smart and good-looking, she thought to herself. With Drew as my mentor, I can do anything at all.

Chapter Two

*A*fter a ten-minute break, Drew was back in the staff room, clipboard in hand and all business.

"Here's the deal, people. We're committed to airing our first show on July Fourth."

Keera gasped. "But Mr. Pearson—I mean, Drew—that's in two weeks!"

Drew grinned. "Right, so I guess you'll have to hustle."

"What kind of show do you want us to put together?" Amanda asked tentatively.

"That's up to all of you," Drew responded. "It's your show. You've got four fifteen-minute segments to fill. You need to figure out what to do with them."

"Just like that?" Hero asked, incredulous.

"Yep. I mean, I'll show you how to work the cameras, mikes, studio and control panels. And I'll be around to help you with the fine points, the editing details, stuff like that. But from this point on, you guys are full-fledged KSS-TV staffers. So, pull together a program proposal. Figure out your stories, and I'll take a look."

The four new staffers just looked at each other in disbelief. None of their teachers had ever let them decide their own assignments. Sure, they all had ideas, but they'd never worked on a television station before. Could they do it?

"This program proposal," Jamar began. "When do you want it?"

"How about later today?" Drew asked.

There was a short silence.

"Sure, Drew, we can do it," Amanda spoke up. She loved the way Drew's name rolled smoothly over her tongue. She felt like she had been born to say his name.

"Great, see you in a while," Drew said, flashing another brilliant smile at Amanda. Then he went into his office, leaving the four of them on their own.

Hero swiveled in his chair, eyeing Amanda with a challenging stare.

"So, since later today is no problem for you, you must already have your piece figured out. What's your story, Amanda?" Hero asked.

Amanda looked at Hero, tossing her hair over her shoulder.

"Well," Amanda started hesitantly. "I had

been thinking about doing a piece on summer fashion, to start. You know, who'll be wearing what at the beach, on the street, and at the Cliffside July Fourth Beach Bash."

For a moment, no one said a thing.

Then Jamar said, "Yeah, sounds great." He plugged in his headset and started thrumming his fingers on the desk.

Amanda turned to Keera. "What do you think?"

"Uh, it could be interesting," Keera replied. She didn't want to hurt Amanda's feelings, even if she was being kind of an airhead.

"Want to know what I think?" Hero asked with a hint of a smile playing around his lips.

"Not really," Amanda replied.

"I think a fashion show is just what Cliffside needs. In fact," Hero said, cupping his hand to his ear, "I can hear the townfolk clamoring for it."

Hero's expression was serious, but his under-lip trembled slightly as he tried not to laugh.

"How would *you* know so much about what people in Cliffside want to watch?" Amanda asked. "You're pretty new in town."

Hero was stung by Amanda's comment. Rich kids always made him feel like an outsider. His neck stained red with the effort of pretending Amanda's remark hadn't hurt him.

Amanda was immediately sorry. She hadn't meant to make Hero feel bad. But, honestly, he was really being a pain and a half. She comforted herself with the knowledge that Drew was sure to approve of her idea.

"What about you, Keera?" Hero asked, turning away from Amanda.

Jamar unplugged his headset. Suddenly, he was all ears.

"Well," Keera began thoughtfully, "I think, since it's summer, and we're going to air on the day of the Beach Bash, maybe I'll do a segment on the beaches. You know, they've closed Cliffside Beach Lagoon, and nobody's said much about why," Keera added.

"Cool idea," Jamar said enthusiastically.

"That is pretty great," Hero admitted.

"And we can tie it in with my beachwear story," Amanda added excitedly.

When Keera looked at her doubtfully, Amanda said, "Or maybe not. Perhaps we shouldn't confuse the audience with too many slants in one segment."

"Good thinking," Hero commented to Amanda.

"Thanks," Amanda said, giving Hero a withering glance.

"I hate to get between you two crazy lovebirds . . ." Jamar said teasingly. "But I'd like to tape my JellyJam band brothers and myself—kind of a way to demonstrate our renowned musical abilities and perhaps become a regular feature to appear on our show. Sound okay to you all?" Jamar asked.

"It sounds like it has potential," Keera said seriously.

"Thanks," Jamar said with a big smile. "I'll take that as a yes." Turning to Hero, Jamar poked him out of his thoughts. "Okay with you, dude?"

"Definitely. Sounds cool," Hero responded evenly. "Maybe you could do some backup music for my piece, too."

"Absolutely. Which is what?" Jamar asked.

"I was thinking maybe a story on the Cliffside High football team. I thought I'd interview the team at summer practice and then do a retrospective of the last few years."

Turning to Amanda, Hero asked, "Mind if we call a truce? I'm betting you know a lot of the guys on the football team. Do you think you could introduce me so I could interview them?"

Somewhat mollified, Amanda said slowly, "Sure, I guess I could."

Amanda wasn't sure how the football team members were going to feel about being interviewed, especially about last year's season. In the past three years, Cliffside hadn't exactly excelled, losing the statewide championship it had held for ten years. It was kind of a sensitive subject, at least for some of the players. Amanda thought of Tyler Scott, the team's quarterback.

Not knowing much about the team's record, Hero misunderstood Amanda's hesitation.

"That is, if it's not too much trouble," Hero commented drily.

Amanda flushed slightly and her violet eyes glittered with annoyance. "I said I could introduce you," she said.

"Great," Hero said in a low voice, looking straight into Amanda's clear eyes. For a brief moment, he imagined his lips gently brushing against Amanda's soft mouth. Then Hero blinked back to reality.

"So, does anyone else have any thoughts on the show before we present our ideas to Drew?" Amanda asked, looking around at the others.

Hero glanced at Keera and Jamar. "Well, to be honest, Amanda, I think you might want to reconsider your fashion show thing," he said slowly.

"Oh, and why is that?" Amanda asked, the hairs on her neck beginning to bristle.

Keera and Jamar just looked at each other, waiting for what Hero had to say next. They both knew Amanda's idea was weak, but neither wanted to address it. After all, Amanda was so sincere. And they hadn't wanted to hurt her feelings on the first day.

Hero knew that Keera and Jamar weren't about to get into it with Amanda. But he also knew that, if he was going to have a job for the whole summer, the first program had to be a killer. And a straight fashion show wasn't going to do it.

"Fashion shows are kind of boring," Hero said. "I mean, what guy in his right mind is going to watch a local fashion show, even if it does hold out the possibility of a few girls in bikinis?"

Hero paused thoughtfully. "I think we've covered three of the four things people watch on television: music videos, sports, and special investigations."

"And what in your expert opinion is the fourth category of interest?" Amanda asked haughtily.

"Comedy."

"Comedy? What am I supposed to do, stand in front of a mike and tell jokes?" Amanda said with contempt.

"Hey, whatever works for you," Hero said.

"You know, Amanda, sometimes fashions can be funny," Keera piped up.

Just then, Drew poked his head in the office. "Hey, folks, I can hear you out here. What's going on?"

Jamar cleared his throat and once again started tapping the table. Keera shifted uncomfortably in her seat. Hero, looking straight ahead at nothing, swiveled from side to side in his chair.

"Amanda?" Drew asked.

With a sidelong glance at Hero, Amanda said, "We're just having a few creative differences, Drew."

"Well, that's fine just so long as you work them out. This is your show. I'll help you, but I'm not going to tell you how to run it. And I'm not going to referee. You're on your own, because I consider us all adults here." Drew smiled encouragingly at them.

Amanda gave Drew an appreciative smile. She'd never known a grown-up who treated her so . . . professionally. Her father still treated her like a little princess. And, of course, her mother never had anything nice to say about her. Amanda's heart warmed toward Drew. Here, finally, was an adult Amanda could trust—someone to whom she could tell her real thoughts.

Drew's voice broke into her reverie.

"So, all suggestions are to be considered carefully and, when possible, included." He lightly tapped Amanda's shoulder and asked, "Are we clear on this, Amanda?"

Amanda's heart skipped a beat at Drew's touch. She looked deeply into his clear blue eyes.

"Definitely. We'll work it all out. Whatever you say, Drew," Amanda assured him.

"Great!" Drew said. "So, give me what you've got so far."

As Amanda, the self-appointed spokesperson, talked animatedly about their show proposal, Hero watched her come alive under Drew's gaze. He would give anything to figure out how to make Amanda look at him like that.

Chapter Three

The next day, Amanda took great pains to dress in a grown-up, professional-looking white linen suit with a lemon yellow silk tank top, which her mother had bought her for some Club function or other.

"Why, Amanda, how pretty. I'm so used to seeing you in those rally jeans and silly shirts, I'd forgotten what you looked like in real clothes," Mrs. Townsend remarked with surprise.

"Thanks a lot, Mom," Amanda replied, stepping lightly into the dining room where her father was breakfasting. Amanda cleared her throat, but her father's face remained buried in his morning newspaper, oblivious to her presence.

Amanda did a little twirl in front of him to get him to notice her.

"So, what do you think, Dad?" Amanda asked, knowing just what her father would say.

Looking up from his newspaper, Mr.

Townsend's face split into a wide grin as he looked at his daughter. "You look beautiful, princess," he responded softly, "as always!" Then he reached over the newspaper to give Amanda a quick hug.

"I mean, what do you think of the outfit? Do I look like a grown-up, professional TV woman?" Amanda wanted to know.

"You'll always look like my little girl to me, no matter what you wear," Mr. Townsend answered, then returned to his reading.

As Amanda sat down at the table, gingerly biting into some buttered toast and pouring herself some orange juice, Mr. Townsend peered over his paper and asked, "Are you going somewhere special today, Amanda?"

"I started my new job yesterday, Dad. Don't you remember? At the KSS-TV cable station," Amanda replied between tiny bites of toast.

Folding the newspaper down, Mr. Townsend looked immediately apologetic. "Of course I remember, I'm just a little distracted this morning. So, how's the job so far?"

"It's okay," Amanda admitted. "The station manager, Drew Pearson, is really cool. I like the other kids working there, too, mostly." Amanda hesitated for a moment, thinking about Hero.

Mrs. Townsend entered the dining room and sat down beside her husband. "Who are the other kids working there?" Mrs. Townsend asked, delicately sipping her black coffee.

"Oh, just some kids from school. Their parents don't belong to the Club or anything, Mom," Amanda said with a slight edge to her voice, "so you wouldn't know them."

"No, I'm sure I wouldn't," Mrs. Townsend replied with a sigh.

Checking her watch, Amanda jumped up from the table, almost knocking over her chair, forgetting for a moment her new dignified status as a professional grown-up.

"I've got to run, or I'm going to be late!" Amanda said.

"Amanda, for goodness sake, be careful!" Mrs. Townsend said sharply.

Amanda gave her father a quick hug and kissed the air above her mother's head.

"Later!" she called and ran out the door.

When Amanda hurried into the KSS-TV station, she saw that everyone was grouped around Drew. They all looked up and stopped what they were doing.

"Amanda, you look wonderful," Keera said. "Are you going somewhere after work?"

Before Amanda could reply, Drew impatiently motioned Amanda over to where they were all standing. Amanda had expected Drew to compliment her on her outfit and grown-up appearance. Instead, after giving her a quick smile, Drew just said, "Hey, Amanda, I'm glad you're here. Now I can get started showing you all how to use the equipment."

Drew went rapidly through the station, giving them a crash course in filming and editing. They all listened attentively while Drew explained how to use the portable cameras and mikes on location, the large, fixed cameras for studio shots, and the lights and wiring they would need to set up.

"Okay, as I said yesterday, each of you is going to have to do it all. You're going to be producer, director, reporter, editor, and cameraman—I mean cameraperson," Drew said with a grin at Keera and Amanda.

"Do we have to do everything by ourselves for our own shows?" Amanda asked, looking doubtfully at the music-mixing panel, where Jamar was nimbly playing with the tracking and mixing functions.

"Well, you'll probably want to work together on your different segments. It's up to you to figure out the best use of your talents," Drew said.

"Hey, I'll be happy to mix the music for everyone's segments!" Jamar offered immediately. "This machine is awesome."

Jamar's enthusiasm was contagious. Amanda immediately turned to Drew and asked, "Do you mind showing me how to use the visual mixer again? I didn't quite get it the first time."

"Mind if I listen in?" Hero asked, glancing at Amanda admiringly. Although Hero knew a lot about rebuilding motorcycles, computer hardware was a whole different story.

"No problem," Drew said, shepherding Amanda and Hero back over to the mixer.

"Say, Keera," Jamar said before she could follow Drew and the others. "I'll work the camera and mikes for your shots, whenever. This way," he grinned widely, "we'll get to spend quality time together, so we can fall madly in love."

"Jamar!" Keera said, blushing furiously.

"I'm serious, Keera—about doing camera work for you, I mean," Jamar added hastily, not wanting to make Keera any more embarrassed than she was.

"Well, I'm probably going to do an interview later in the week with one of my favorite teachers, Mr. Moss."

"Mr. Moss is a favorite teacher of yours?" Jamar asked incredulously.

"Yes," Keera said seriously. "He knows an awful lot about local marine life and ocean conditions. Why do you sound so amazed?"

Jamar shook his head. Maybe his friend Rogue was right and this girl did breathe air from a different planet.

"Because Mr. Moss is very possibly the most uptight, unfunniest dude I have ever had the bad luck to encounter," Jamar said. "The man has no imagination. I mean, I gave him the best of my work, and the creep told me that music and marine life just didn't mingle."

"What are you talking about?" Keera asked.

"For my end-of-term project, instead of doing a boring report on some fish, I composed some music, using whale songs in the background. And the guy gave me a *D-*!"

"Listen, Jamar. Mr. Moss is one of the smartest teachers at Cliffside High. Maybe he just thought that you were trying to get out of doing the work," Keera said.

"Really," Jamar said unhappily, sighing

the sigh of the misunderstood composer. Seeing Keera's serious expression, he thought, this chick needs to lighten up. "Well, maybe a whale rap song wasn't what he was after," Jamar joked, hoping to see Keera's frown turn into a smile.

Keera didn't know what to think. Jamar didn't seem to take anything seriously. She knew he wasn't exactly Type A, but getting a D- wasn't something to joke about. In Keera's family, anything less than an A- was the basis for a serious discussion. Keera didn't even want to contemplate what a D-, or someone who got one, would inspire.

"Forget it, Keera. He's a genius, I'm a goof-off. I shouldn't have messed around. Can we move on?" Jamar asked.

"I guess so," Keera said slowly.

"Great," Jamar bubbled up again. "So, I can make it later in the week. Just tell me where and when, and I'm there!"

Keera nodded, smiling at Jamar's eagerness in spite of herself. He was so *happy*, so genuinely full of feeling good, that it bubbled up out of his eyes and made everyone around him smile when he spoke.

Jamar finally tore himself away from the music mixer, and he and Keera went out in the main room to see what Hero and Amanda were up to.

Hero was jotting down some notes at his desk. Amanda and Drew were still working on the visual mixer.

"Okay, Amanda, let's go through it again," Drew said patiently, as though he had all the time in the world.

"I'm sorry it's taking so long for me to get this," Amanda said.

"No problem," Drew said with an easy smile. "We'll take as much time as you need and get it right." Drew slipped his arm around her shoulder briefly to bring her closer to the controls.

Happily, Amanda turned her attention to the panel, basking in Drew's calm warmth and gentle manner.

As Amanda listened again to the way the mixing worked, an idea began to percolate about how to make her fashion segment into a comedy. She returned to her desk, lost in thought, unaware that Hero's eyes followed her closely, drinking in what he saw. Hero was positive that nowhere in the world was there anyone as beautiful as Amanda. It was obvious she had it all. So what could she ever see in someone like him?

"Hey, everybody, I just came up with another angle for my story!" Amanda said.

"Acute or obtuse?" Hero asked kiddingly.

Ignoring Hero, Amanda called Drew over to listen to her new idea. "Here's my plan," Amanda began. "Instead of doing just a straight look at clothes for the summer, I thought maybe it would perk up things if I did a comparison-type thing. I could look critically at what fashion designers want us to wear versus what is really practical and comfortable."

As she warmed to her subject, Amanda's words tumbled out quickly.

"Now that I finally understand how the visual mixer works, I thought I'd contrast fashion clips with real people on the street, showing what works and what doesn't in a funny way," she finished triumphantly.

Hero couldn't believe it. Amanda had actually taken his suggestions to heart.

"That's excellent, Amanda," Drew said admiringly. "A really fresh approach."

"I can come up with some great music for something like that," Jamar offered.

"That would be great," Amanda said.

"I'll help with the modeling and costumes, if you want me to," Keera added shyly.

Amanda gave Keera a grateful smile.

"And I think we have some stock footage on this season's designer fashion shows— you know, some of the really bizarre stuff that comes out of Paris," Drew offered.

"Thanks, Drew," Amanda said, touching him lightly on the arm. "I couldn't have come up with a new plan if it hadn't been for you."

The skin on Hero's neck and face flushed against his black cotton T-shirt. He couldn't believe that Amanda was thanking Drew when Hero was the one who had suggested a humorous approach.

Who was he kidding? He, of all people, should know that rich girls like Amanda and guys like him couldn't ever make it together. Look at how unhappy his parents' marriage had turned out.

Just this morning, they'd been fighting again.

"There's an opening at the local dress shop for a saleswoman," Mrs. Montoya remarked casually. "I was thinking of going in and applying for it."

"My wife doesn't need to work," Mr. Montoya insisted. "We've managed so far, and Hero is doing his share."

"It would be nice to have a little extra to buy some pretty things for the house and to be able to put some money away for school for Hero . . ." Mrs. Montoya said, trailing off when she saw the anger on her husband's face.

"I'm not a rich man like your father, and I

never will be. The house looks fine without pretty knickknacks like your mother had. And Hero is a poor man's son. He's not going to any fancy colleges. We'll make do the way we are," Mr. Montoya said, angrily pushing his chair back from the table.

"Joseph, I'm not talking about being rich. I'm talking about making things nicer," she called to his departing back as he stormed out the kitchen door and threw himself into his pickup truck.

Mrs. Montoya placed her hand gently on Hero's shoulder, tears rolling slowly down her cheeks.

"He's such an angry man. What do you think I should do?" she asked Hero quietly.

Just then, Amanda placed her hand lightly on Hero's shoulder, interrupting his unhappy thoughts.

"So, what do you think of my new idea?" Amanda asked, leaning toward him. She really wanted to know.

Hero blinked back to the present. For a moment, Amanda had looked just like his mother.

"Why ask me?" Hero replied coolly, although his heart was thumping at Amanda's closeness. "Drew told you it was 'excellent.'" Hero attempted an imitation of

Drew. "So it's fine," Hero said evenly. Then he turned to riffle through some papers on his desk.

"Fine," Amanda snapped, turning on her heel and heading for Drew's office to talk about that stock footage he'd mentioned.

Hero's gaze followed Amanda as she stalked past him. His eyes lingered over her tall, slim frame moving gracefully in the white linen suit. The scent of her freshly washed hair still hung in the air about him.

Out of the corner of her eye, Keera spotted Hero's gaze. His handsome face was filled with longing, like a kid with no change standing outside the window of a candy store, his nose pressed up against the glass.

Snapping out of his reverie, Hero abruptly pushed back his chair and got up.

"I'm going out for a while to try the portable camera. I'll bring the equipment back later today," Hero announced to no one in particular. Shouldering the camera, Hero banged out of the room.

Hero's Harley roared away from the station. He seemed awfully angry all of a sudden, and Keera couldn't imagine why.

"Why the puzzled look?" Jamar asked Keera.

"Oh, nothing," Keera said, not really able

to put into words what was going through her mind. She was surprised that Jamar had been able to read the expression on her face. And she was surprised that he would care enough to ask.

"Something I said?" Jamar asked.

Keera blushed slightly. "No, Jamar, it's nothing you said. Do you think Hero's mad about something?" she asked. "He seemed sort of upset when he left."

"No way, he's just the silent, moody type. Handsome guys are always like that. Not like me. I'm always working on getting my personality out there before you take a good look!" Jamar joked. "Don't you start falling for Hero—you haven't even given me a chance yet!"

Keera blushed again, her mocha-colored cheeks turning a deep rose.

"Get out of here, Jamar," Keera said, ducking her head and turning her attention back to her paperwork.

Keera wasn't used to flirting. And she didn't know whether or not to believe that Jamar was interested in her. He was definitely cute, and very funny.

For a moment, Keera imagined Jamar, in his black and purple bike shorts, headset, and bright green tank top, meeting her stolid, conservative, schoolteacher parents.

She nearly burst into giggles at the thought of her mother's apoplectic expression.

"Hey, I'm not joking," Jamar told her earnestly. "I really do want a chance with you, Keera, to show you I'm not just a goofball musician," he added, placing his hand on her arm and looking deeply into her eyes.

Just then, Amanda came back into the main room. Flustered, Keera quickly withdrew her arm from Jamar's touch. She picked up a pencil and peered down at her work, trying to focus on the words on the page.

Jamar glanced over at the clock above the door.

"Uh-oh, gotta go, ladies," Jamar said, remembering he had promised to meet Rogue and the boys to rehearse for their upcoming videotaping session. "Later for you all," he called as he raced out of the station, plugging in his headset as he went. He stumbled over a chair and bumped into a desk corner before he finally made it out the door.

Amanda and Keera giggled at Jamar's awkward exit.

"Jamar's kind of cute, don't you think?" Amanda asked.

"He's okay," Keera replied shyly. Keera didn't usually confide her real feelings to anyone other than her best friend, Jeanette. And the aura of popularity that surrounded Amanda made Keera feel uncomfortable talking to her about anything other than work.

"He sure thinks you are," Amanda said breezily. "And he's very funny," she added.

Keera blushed. Amanda continued, not seeming to notice Keera's discomfort.

"Jamar's a whole lot nicer than Hero, I think," Amanda said.

"Oh, I don't know."

"Definitely," Amanda said emphatically.

Then, quickly changing the subject, Amanda drew closer to Keera and said in a whisper, "Don't you think Drew is the most wonderful guy you've ever met?"

Keera hesitated a moment. "He's great, but he's kind of old, isn't he?" she asked.

"Oh, he's not so old. Maybe twenty-five or twenty-six. I mean, at least he's still under thirty!" Amanda said. "And he's so understanding and wise. He's promised to spend some extra time with me going over that fashion footage he was talking about before. Isn't that great?" Amanda asked, without really listening for Keera's response. All she could think of was how wonderful it would be to work closely with Drew.

Keera just nodded. She was thinking about Jamar. In spite of her doubts about him, Keera was looking forward to taping the Moss interview with Jamar. Who knows? Maybe Jamar had really meant what he said about wanting a chance with her. Stranger things had happened, although, Keera thought wryly, not in her life.

Chapter Four

$\mathcal{A}$ few days later, Amanda and Keera were working in the office. Neither Hero nor Jamar had been around much lately. Hero was out at the library researching the Cliffside High football stats for the past ten years, and Jamar was busy rehearsing with his band.

Keera was agonizing over today's interview with Mr. Moss for her segment, which she'd titled "Operation Cliffside."

This was going to be Keera's first ever appearance in front of a television camera, and she and her mother had haunted the discount stores and sale racks in every store in the Cliffside County area, laboring over what Keera was going to wear.

Finally, they had come up with something that Keera thought would work: a medium-length navy blue skirt with an ivory-colored silk scoop-necked shirt. It wasn't exactly an Amanda original, Keera thought, remembering the parade of beautiful outfits that

Amanda had sported that week, but, then, she wasn't Amanda.

"Keera, would you be able to help me model and videotape some of the outfits I've got planned for the show?" Amanda asked, breaking into Keera's thoughts.

"Sure, Amanda," Keera said. She liked Amanda a lot, and she was happy that they were becoming friends. Keera also couldn't wait to see what kind of fashion statements Amanda was planning to spoof on the show.

"I'm going to spend the weekend putting together stuff. Why don't you come over to my house early next week? By then I'll have all the clothes assembled, and we can take turns modeling and shooting," Amanda suggested.

Then, Amanda added happily, "Today, Drew and I are having a lunch meeting to lay out the canned fashion footage he's got."

Keera noticed how Amanda's cheeks flushed and her eyes sparkled when she talked about Drew. She wished someone would have that effect on her.

"Next week is perfect for me," Keera said. "I'm meeting Jamar at noon at the beach today to shoot the lagoon scenes and interview Mr. Moss. After that, I'll just have editing and background music to worry about."

"Great," Amanda said with a grin. Keera wasn't like any of her other friends. She was never catty, never made snippy remarks about people's clothes or their looks.

Amanda looked up at the clock. It was 11:45.

"Keera, what time did you say you were meeting Jamar?" Amanda asked.

"Ohmigosh," Keera said, checking the clock. She jumped up from her chair and stuffed her papers into her knapsack. "I lost all track of time, working on these questions," Keera said nervously. "I told Jamar we'd set up the equipment at noon. Mr. Moss is meeting us at 12:30. I better get going," Keera said, rushing around, picking up the portable camera and equipment bag.

"Talk to you later!" Amanda called after Keera's departing back.

Keera hurriedly threw her papers and the equipment bag into her mother's car. Then she drove to Cliffside Lagoon, where she and Jamar had arranged to meet. It was only a little after noon when she arrived.

Spotting Jamar's bicycle in the parking lot, Keera parked the car, grabbed her papers, awkwardly slipped the bag on her shoulders, and headed for the shore.

There she saw Jamar, alone on the cordoned-off lagoon beach, in a world by himself, tossing rocks into the ocean waves that lapped against the sandy dunes separating the lagoon from the rest of the ocean. Just like Keera's little brother, Jamar smiled with pleasure each time a rock skipped three times before sinking into the waves.

Watching Jamar, in his cut-off jeans and ripped T-shirt, splash and run in the foamy ocean surf, Keera felt something stir inside her. He was so lighthearted, so . . . free.

I wonder what it's like to feel as though there's nothing you have to do, no place you need to be, and nowhere you have to go, Keera thought to herself.

Keera always had something to do. There was schoolwork, babysitting, chores at home, and now there was her work at KSS. Keera's parents believed in establishing responsibility young. They had set their goals high for Keera, and she had always believed there was no other way to live her life. In fact, nothing before this moment had ever seemed more appealing.

Nothing, that is, until . . . Jamar.

Jamar turned to see Keera watching him from the sandy ridge above the lagoon. Jamar laughed at her, daring her to come in and get her feet wet.

When she wouldn't come, he came over and tried to pull Keera in. Protesting with laughter, Keera let the equipment bag slip from her shoulder and permitted Jamar to drag her almost to the shoreline, where she dug in her heels and pulled away.

Surprised, Jamar let go, and Keera fell solidly on the wet sand. Stunned and distraught that her interview outfit was ruined, Keera struggled to stand up and examine the damage.

Jamar rushed over and knelt beside her.

"Oh, Keera, I'm so sorry. I didn't mean for you to fall like that."

Jamar scooped her up off the sand as though she weighed nothing at all. He set Keera upright and searched her face to make sure that she wasn't mad and that she really was all right. His tender concern made Keera's heart ache.

Jamar lightly brushed the sand from her arms, from her back, from her hair. Keera stood perfectly still, afraid to move—afraid that if she did, it would somehow break the spell.

Then Jamar slowly leaned closer, looking straight into Keera's eyes, head tilted toward the side. Jamar righted the wire-rimmed frames on her nose, which had gotten knocked crooked when she fell.

At his touch, time stopped. Keera felt like something deep inside was melting. As

Jamar came closer and closer, Keera held her breath, feeling his hand on her cheek.

"Ahem." Someone cleared his throat loudly from behind them.

Jamar and Keera looked around, blinking.

"Ms. Johnson, I believe we said 12:30 sharp for our interview, did we not?" a voice called from the sandy ridge above the water. "Well, it's about that now, and I'm between summer school classes. May we get started?"

Burning with embarrassment, Keera quickly smoothed down her hair and clothes, averted her eyes from Jamar, and scrambled up the sandy embankment, mumbling her apologies to Mr. Moss.

Jamar sighed. His hands hung limply at his sides. He'd been so close to the sweetest moment of his life, just inches away from kissing Keera's soft, full mouth. Closing his eyes against the sea breeze, he could almost feel her body pressing against his.

"Jamar, could you set up the camera now? We're ready to go," Keera called, all business, pointing to the equipment bag on the sand. There wasn't a trace of the softness of a moment ago.

Following Keera up the ridge, Jamar moved about mechanically, attaching wires, setting up the tripod, the mike.

Surprised to see Jamar and Keera together, Mr. Moss said quietly, "Nice to see you again, Mr. Williams. Working on another musical marine project, perhaps?"

Face burning at the caustic remark, Jamar glanced over at Keera to see what she was thinking. But Keera had her back to him, as if she was purposely refusing to meet his eye.

Keera started the interview, and Mr. Moss drily and unemotionally answered Keera's questions about the destroyed marine life; the local manufacturers, like Scott Enterprises, who were contributing to the problem; and the future of the tidepools and the lagoon. Mr. Moss summed up his interview with a deadpan prediction of gloom and doom, explaining how the pollution would eventually affect everyone, animals and people alike.

Listening to Mr. Moss, Jamar felt sick to his stomach. He had walked around the lagoon before Keera had arrived. He'd seen the sand beside the oversized storm drainpipes stained by oil spots and chemical waste, littered with trash.

Without knowing any of the scientific details, Jamar could see the mess that was being created, and he was angry. This was the lagoon where he and his friends had played pirates when he was a kid. Now it wasn't even fit for sea slugs.

He couldn't bear to hear Moss talk about the inevitable destruction of the beach in such a matter-of-fact way. Turning to Keera, Jamar signaled cut. Flipping off the camera, Jamar waved her over and said, "I've got to split. Can you take over here? It's all set up. Just flip the switch and keep talking." Jamar showed her. Then he walked away.

Seeing the startled look in Keera's eyes, he knew that she was getting the wrong idea. But Jamar couldn't do anything about that right now, not in front of Mr. Moss.

"Ms. Johnson, since Mr. Williams seems to be in such a hurry to depart, can I assume that we're done, too?" Mr. Moss asked.

Maintaining an aura of control, Keera replied, "No, just a few more questions, Mr. Moss. I've got the camera ready to roll."

After a few minutes, the interview was over, and Keera thanked Mr. Moss for his time. Mr. Moss had always been perfectly pleasant to Keera in the past. But the way he'd treated Jamar, and, for that matter, the way he'd treated Keera for being with Jamar, had annoyed her.

It's true, Mr. Moss was a very intelligent, academically gifted man—but academics weren't everything, were they? Keera wondered. Sometimes it was okay just to let loose and have fun, wasn't it? Then she caught herself. Before today, she'd never considered anything other than academics important. What was happening to her?

Keera's cheeks burned at the memory of Jamar's touch, the look of concern in his eyes, the way he had scooped her up from the sand.

But then he had simply walked away in the middle of her interview. What kind of person would do something like that? Keera asked herself, puzzled and angry at the same time.

She could almost hear her mother's voice saying, "A no-good, lazy, shiftless musician, that's what!"

As she packed up the equipment, Keera looked down at her watch. Almost 3:30. I wonder how Amanda's lunch with Drew went, Keera thought.

When Keera entered the station, she saw Amanda and Drew huddled over the visual mixer control panel together, looking as if no one else in the world mattered.

Amanda glanced over at Keera. She flashed her a quick, happy smile, then turned her attention immediately back to Drew.

"See you in the morning," Keera called

after putting the portable camera and mikes back in their places.

She wasn't sure that Amanda and Drew even noticed that she'd spoken.

Amanda was having a wonderful time. This was her first ever working lunch date, and it had been everything she'd hoped—almost.

At first, Amanda had thought that she and Drew would go out to lunch at some elegant dining spot, maybe Top of the Cliff, to talk about how to use the footage. But Drew ordered in sandwiches so that they could eat and work at the same time.

It wasn't fancy and formal, but Amanda had still felt very grown-up as Drew showed her how to cut and splice the different fashion shots and then called for a twenty-minute break so they could eat and talk.

Drew asked Amanda about school and about her family, and Amanda found herself chattering about her mother's obsession with the Yacht Club, and how her dad was always busy at work. Amanda talked about Kit, her thirteen-year-old sister, and what a pain she was—and Drew just laughed, as if he knew exactly what Amanda was talking about.

The whole time, Drew listened attentively, never taking his eyes from Amanda's face. Amanda's eyes sparkled, the color rising on her cheeks.

Amanda knew she had been right about Drew. Finally, here was someone she could talk to, someone who didn't have an agenda of his own. And Drew had singled her out for his special attention!

Before Amanda knew it, the twenty minutes had flown by, and Drew smoothly turned their attention back to the monitor. Amanda scolded herself for not asking Drew about himself. Next time, we'll talk about him, Amanda promised herself.

And, maybe, next time, the setting would be a little more romantic.

Chapter Five

*T*he next morning, Amanda and Keera teamed up to comb the thrift stores and local boutiques for accessories to go with Amanda's outfits. Amanda knew lots of great places to shop for outlandish and out-of-the-ordinary stuff, while Keera knew where to find discount designer outlets. They agreed that together they made an impressive fashion investigative team.

While they were out "researching," Jamar and Hero were working at the station. Hero was glancing over his interview questions for the football team. Amanda had told him to meet her at the football field this afternoon, and she would introduce him to the team. Jamar was fiddling around on the music mixer, trying to fine-tune one of the new songs he'd written.

Hero walked over and knocked on the thick glass of the music control room, and Jamar waved him in.

"Would you come on location with me

and work the camera today? I'm meeting Amanda over at the football field. Summer practice starts today, and I want to get some live footage in addition to last year's clips," Hero said.

"No problem," Jamar said, jotting down some notes before shutting off the music mixer.

Twenty minutes later, Jamar and Hero roared up to the practice field. Amanda was already there, laughing and talking to her best friend, Samantha Walker, leader of the cheerleading squad. The cheerleaders, in their perky lavender skirts and shiny gold stretch tops, were out on the field practicing, too—and checking out the team at the same time.

When Hero's motorcycle roared up, everyone on the field stopped what they were doing to stare at Hero and Jamar. In his carefully ripped jeans and close-fitting T-shirt, Hero again felt like an outsider from another planet. But he played it cool, calmly surveying the football field and the guys in their pads and jerseys.

"Jamar—Hero, over here!" Amanda called, waving to them from the other side of the field.

Amanda looked perfect, as usual, in her babydoll sundress, with a big-flowered hair clip and black Doc Martens. Her blonde hair framed her beautiful face, reflecting a halo of sunshine around her, which shimmered when she changed position. Hero blinked at the sight, forgetting for a moment that he and Amanda didn't really get along.

"I was wondering when you guys were going to show up," Amanda said. "The coach has already started the team on practice plays, so you'll probably have to wait until they take a break."

"That's all right with me," Jamar said. "I've got to set up the camera stuff anyway."

"Hey, Jamar, how about shooting the practice plays now, and we'll see if we can use the footage?" Hero suggested.

"Sure," Jamar said agreeably, moving offside to set up the camera and get the microphone ready.

Hero and Amanda stood together awkwardly for a moment.

"Thanks for setting this up, Amanda," Hero said in a low voice, stepping just a bit closer. He could smell her light perfume.

"No problem," Amanda said to Hero, looking up at him.

Her breath caught. After the first day, Amanda had ceased to notice how good-looking Hero was. Most of the time her thoughts were filled with Drew. But here, out on the football field, Amanda took a good, long look at Hero again.

Amanda noticed how his silky brown hair fell across his forehead in the wind, and the intensity of his deep brown eyes. His chest muscles rippled against the cloth of his shirt when he moved. Through the ragged slits in his jeans, she could see the well-defined muscles right above his knees and the soft, curly brown down that probably covered his whole leg. Amanda blushed.

"Amanda, aren't you going to introduce me to your friend?" Samantha asked sweetly, coming up to where Amanda was standing with Hero and squeezing herself between them.

"Oh, sure," Amanda said, remembering suddenly that Samantha had thought Hero was cute. "Hero Montoya, this is my best friend, Samantha Walker. Hero works with me at KSS, Samantha," Amanda explained.

"He does? I didn't think anyone but you and Drew worked at KSS. At least, not from the way you go on about him. It's always Drew this and Drew that," Samantha teased.

Amanda looked a little embarrassed and quickly changed the subject. For some reason she didn't want to talk about her feelings for Drew in front of Hero.

"Hero's doing a sports spot for the first show," Amanda explained.

"Well, you know, Hero, cheerleading's a sport, too. And we cheerleaders are very athletic," Samantha added, putting her hand on Hero's hard chest. "Oooh, and so are you," Samantha cooed.

Amanda sighed. Sometimes Samantha could be so outrageous. But it sure didn't look as though Hero minded Samantha's attention. Realizing that sent a little stab of pain through Amanda's heart. Now why would I care whether or not Hero likes Samantha? Amanda wondered.

Samantha's voice broke into Amanda's thoughts.

"Maybe you'd like to put the cheerleaders on your show. I'm always available for an interview with you," Samantha gushed, moving closer to Hero so that their arms almost touched.

As Samantha continued speaking, Hero hid his discomfort in an offhand expression that some people mistook for interest. To himself he was thinking, I knew it was a mistake to get mixed up with Amanda and her friends. This girl Samantha was about as appealing as a walking, talking Kewpie doll. Hero smiled slightly at the comparison.

Samantha took Hero's smile for encouragement and continued talking, reaching over every so often to touch him lightly on the shoulder.

Moving subtly out of Samantha's touching range, Hero nodded politely, letting her stream of chatter wash over him without bothering to listen. His eye caught Amanda's, and, for a moment, he could swear she'd looked almost . . . annoyed at the attention he was paying to Samantha.

Before Hero could consider this development, Jamar called out, "Camera's ready to go, dude."

"Nice to meet you, Samantha," Hero said quickly. "Catch you later, Amanda. And thanks," Hero added warmly, wanting Amanda to know he really appreciated her aid.

"Glad to help," Amanda told him sincerely. Then she smiled at him.

Hero smiled back. For the second time since they met, Amanda noticed how great Hero looked when he smiled.

As he caught the genuine interest in Amanda's eyes, Hero's heart leaped. Maybe he still had a chance with Amanda after all.

Hero trotted offside to the fifty-yard line where Jamar had set up the equipment. Next to Jamar stood a middle-aged man with a slight paunch and a kindly manner, peering out from under his Cliffside High sports cap brim.

"Hello there, son, I'm Coach Watson. You must be Hero Montoya, the KSS-TV reporter fellow. Amanda told me you'd be by."

Coach Watson held out his hand and Hero shook it firmly.

"I have that starting list of players for you right here," the Coach said. "It's hot off the press, if you know what I mean."

Hero glanced briefly at the list.

"Hero, I shot the practice plays. Ready to roll on the interviews when you are," Jamar informed him.

The Coach called for a fifteen-minute break, then ambled toward the locker room.

Tyler Scott sauntered over to check out Hero and to make himself available for an interview. He and Hero were the same height, six feet tall. But, somehow, Hero seemed more solid and steady, while Tyler was thin and hard-edged.

In a football jersey instead of his usual khakis and Ralph Lauren polo, Tyler looked out of context. His nasal voice combined with his superior attitude was enough to irritate most people. Hero was no exception.

"So, you're the new guy working with Amanda this summer, huh?" Tyler asked in his superior voice. "Funny, from the way Amanda talked about you, I thought you'd be . . . different."

"Oh?" Hero said coolly, pretending not to care.

Their eyes locked. In that moment, they both knew that friendship wasn't an option.

"My name's Hero Montoya," Hero said abruptly, wanting to get down to business.

"I'm Tyler Scott."

Tyler waited for some show of admiration, respect, envy, recognition—anything. But since Hero was new in town, he didn't know about Scott Enterprises, one of the largest corporate entities in Cliffside. Even if he had, Hero wasn't the type to care.

"Oh, yeah, you're the—uh . . . What's your position, again?" Hero asked.

"In Cliffside? Sole heir to the multi-million-dollar Scott Enterprises. Is that what you mean?" Tyler asked nastily.

Hero looked straight into Tyler's cold blue eyes. "Does being the sole heir to a fortune help you out on the field?" Hero asked with mock innocence.

"Yeah, it does. And everywhere else in Cliffside, too, as you'll soon find out," Tyler replied, stalking off toward Amanda and Samantha, both of whom greeted Tyler affectionately.

Immediately Hero wished he had kept his mouth shut. He had just started to make some progress with Amanda. Now, after insulting this obnoxious friend of hers, he'd be lower than dirt once again.

Then he checked the coach's list of the starting lineup and realized that Tyler Scott wasn't even on it. Hero shrugged.

Jamar started the camera rolling, and Hero asked the players about their new strategies, how they felt about last season, and what would be different about this one.

The guys chatted up the usual line about this being a winning year and looking forward to recapturing the state championship. Then Hero went over to the guy whose name was listed as the starting quarterback. But he hung back, saying nothing at all. Nobody wanted to talk much about the last few years.

After Hero had spoken to each of the guys, gotten their names, and given them a chance to mug for the camera, he called to Jamar to wrap it up. From the corner of his eye, he noticed Tyler standing between Amanda and Samantha, talking intently.

Amanda was listening and smiling, her head bent toward Tyler companionably, as though they'd known each other forever.

Hero's heart sank. Just when he thought

he'd made some small progress with Amanda, he had to screw it up by getting into it with Tyler. He hadn't realized that Tyler and Amanda were such good friends. For a moment he wondered if they were even more.

"Hey, Hero. Don't you want to interview the quarterback?" Tyler asked. "Maybe get a shot of me holding the ball or leaping to catch it, like so . . ." Tyler mugged for the girls, making Samantha giggle and Amanda smile.

Holding up the starting list that the coach had given him, Hero said innocently, "I only have enough time for the starting players."

Tyler froze. His eyes narrowed.

"I *am* the starting quarterback," Tyler told Hero coldly.

"Not according to this," Hero shot back.

His face suffused with anger, Tyler replied, "It must be tough to be new in town and such a slow study. But you'll catch on to how things work in Cliffside sooner or later."

Samantha gazed up at Tyler and giggled adoringly. Tyler smiled his supercilious smile.

Hero's temper boiled close to the surface. Everything around Tyler faded to gray. Hero's expression turned to stone, and his eyes went blank. Every muscle in his body was straining to punch out Tyler and wipe that silly smile off his face.

Then Hero felt a cool, firm hand on his shoulder.

"Come on, man. It's a wrap. We're out of here," Jamar said in a low tone.

At first, Hero didn't budge. Jamar nodded to a couple of the team members, who had begun to meander over to where Tyler stood.

Hero's eyes narrowed as he observed the team members lining up alongside Tyler. Tyler returned Hero's look with a menacingly icy glare.

"Hey, guys. No reason to get Neanderthal about this," Amanda said in a conciliatory tone, stepping between them. "I mean, maybe the coach made a mistake, Tyler. After all, Hero didn't make up the list. He was just reading from it," Amanda said defensively.

Hero's face grew darker. But this time it was Amanda he turned to in fury.

"This conversation is between Tyler and me, Amanda. It's got nothing to do with you," Hero said in a low, angry voice, his face flushing hotly.

"That's right, Amanda. Don't you think Motorcycle Boy here can take care of himself?" Tyler asked.

Several burly members of the team guffawed at Tyler's remark.

"I can take care of you, if you're interested in finding out," Hero said coolly.

"Oh, is that so?" Tyler hooted, as the team members closed ranks around him. Samantha tittered nervously, moving to stand behind Tyler.

Instinctively, Amanda moved closer to Hero, putting her hand on his arm. Much to her surprise, Amanda's fingers tingled at the contact between her skin and his.

Hero paused. Amanda's touch was like an electric shock bolting through his arm.

"Let it go, Hero," Amanda pleaded.

Hero's eyes hardened. He shrugged off her hand.

"Back off, Amanda. I told you, this doesn't concern you," Hero muttered.

Amanda's face flushed bright red.

"What are you waiting for, Motorcycle Boy?" Tyler taunted. "Afraid?"

Hero's body tensed. He was ready to fight Tyler right here and now.

"Pick your fights, dude. This isn't the time and it's definitely not the place," Jamar said softly.

Looking around, Hero knew Jamar was right. It was suicide to take on Tyler and the football team. It took all of Hero's self-control to pull himself out of the attack mode.

Turning on his heels, without so much as a "Later" to Amanda, Hero headed for his motorcycle with Jamar right behind him. They both hopped onto the bike and roared off.

After Hero and Jamar had gone, Tyler barked out a sharp laugh. Samantha giggled uncertainly, looking from Tyler to Amanda.

Amanda turned on Tyler and Samantha in a fury.

"Why did you treat him like that? You had no right to embarrass him that way. Hero was just doing his job—you know, something some people have to do to earn their money," Amanda said bitingly.

"Hey, keep me out of this," Samantha said, stepping back out of the line of fire. "I was nice to him. In fact, I already told you I think he's kind of cute," Samantha added, looking to see how Tyler would react.

Tyler ignored Samantha. He looked directly at Amanda, wondering just what was going on between her and Hero.

"What are you getting so worked up about?" Tyler asked. "You told me you barely knew this guy, and now you're giving me a hard time because I decided to teach him some manners! He needed a lesson.

Look at the way he treated you! Get real, Amanda. Don't pull a mood swing on me."

Then Tyler stalked off toward the locker room. It was time to have a talk with Coach Watson about the new list of starting players.

Back at the station, Hero and Jamar studiously avoided discussing what had gone on at the football field. Jamar put on his headphones and went back to mixing his music.

Hero started flipping through the copies of old newspaper clips he'd collected, reading them more closely than he had before. It was then that he realized that Tyler Scott had been starting quarterback for the past three seasons, even as a freshman, which was really unusual. Tyler had been replaced every year mid-season, until Cliffside squeaked into the championship. Then, for some reason, Tyler started at quarterback in every game of the championship. Some people speculated that Cliffside lost the championship because Tyler started every game.

That explains why no one on the team wanted to talk about last year's games, Hero thought to himself. But why would an okay guy like the coach keep putting Tyler

Scott in the game if he knew Cliffside was going to lose? Even if Tyler was the heir to Scott Enterprises, what did that have to do with football?

Sifting through the newspaper clips for a clue, Hero happened to notice a short article that had made its way into the pile, even though it wasn't really about the games.

In the last three years, Scott Enterprises had contributed over $75,000 to Cliffside High, making it the most prosperous, well-funded high school in the county. The Scott donation paid for computers, library funding, and the newly renovated football field, track, and gymnastics equipment.

Well, that explains why Tyler gets to play quarterback, even if he stinks, Hero thought, his face burning once more at the memory of his altercation with Tyler.

"Hey, Jamar, did you know that the Scott family gave Cliffside High the money to pay for the new football field and a whole bunch of other stuff?" Hero asked him.

"Yeah, his daddy owns the school and half the town," Jamar answered calmly and shrugged. "So, what of it?"

"Well, Tyler Scott and his daddy don't own the cable station," Hero said, his eyes glowing with excitement as an idea began to form.

"Don't be too sure. Who knows where Drew gets the money to run this place?" Jamar answered. Then, eyeing Hero more closely, Jamar asked, "What do you have in mind?"

"I'll show you later," Hero replied, "once I see if there's any footage that I can use."

Chapter Six

*L*ater that week, Keera was working in the control room, going over all of her accumulated footage. With the July Fourth deadline looming, Keera wanted to splice her shots together so that Jamar would have time to write the background music.

But Keera found her thoughts wandering further and further from the subject of Cliffside Lagoon's pollution and marine life. Instead of the images of the beach, Keera kept seeing herself and Jamar standing by the shore, looking deeply into each other's eyes.

A glitch on one of the monitors abruptly caught Keera's attention. The interruption made her remember how upset she'd been that Jamar had left her hanging just before the end of the interview. How could she even think about getting involved with someone as unreliable and irresponsible as Jamar? They were polar opposites. Her parents would never approve. And her friends would think she'd taken leave of her senses.

But Keera shivered, remembering his fingers gently stroking her hair and the loving look in his eyes as he bent closer toward her.

Suddenly, a door closed behind her, making her jump. Looking around, Keera saw it was Jamar. Not knowing what to say, Keera busied herself with her work.

"Hey, Keera," Jamar said breezily. He was hoping that Keera wasn't still angry about the way he'd left her on the beach. He hadn't had much of a chance to talk to her since that day. Jamar didn't exactly know how to explain that Mr. Moss's matter-of-fact attitude had made him feel sick. And he didn't want to get into a discussion about Mr. Moss again, that was for sure.

"Oh, hi," Keera said distantly, giving him a quick nod, then turning back to her monitor.

"Uh, Keera," Jamar began, sounding more serious than usual.

Keera waited expectantly, not moving. The skin on the back of her neck tingled. Keera wasn't sure whether or not she wanted Jamar to say something about what had happened between them on the beach before Mr. Moss arrived. But maybe saying something, anything, was better than pretending it had never happened.

Just then the station door opened again. Five guys carrying instruments, music, and electronic equipment spilled into the room, filling up all the available space with their instruments and their voices. If Jamar had been planning to say anything about the other day, it would obviously have to wait.

Keera stared at Jamar's friends. They stared back, each examining the other as though they were aliens from Mars. Jamar's friends had quite a presence, in their collection of overalls and muscle shirts, bandannas and caps, baggy shorts and oversized shirts.

"Hey, boys of the JellyJam band, this is a special lady, Keera Johnson. She works here, too," Jamar said, introducing her to every member of the band.

Rogue Jelsen, Jamar's best friend and the lead singer, lifted up his dark shades and gave Keera a frank, open stare.

"So, you're the reason the Jammin' man here spends his days working behind a camera instead of behind the keyboard writing for the band," Rogue said in a voice tinged with resentment.

"Who, me?" Keera barely squeaked out, not knowing exactly what to say.

"Okay, Rogue—guys, the recording studio is down the hall. Let's do it," Jamar urged them. "Keera, would you help set up the cameras while I get these good men into recording mode?" Jamar asked charmingly.

Keera hesitated a moment. At least three nasty comments about leaving her high and dry on the beach while doing her camera work were on the tip of her tongue. But Jamar smiled so sweetly, his eyes shining right at her, that the remarks died in the back of her throat.

"Okay, but . . ." Keera reluctantly agreed.

"Want to stay a while and listen to us?" Jamar asked eagerly. Then seeing the hesitation on Keera's face, he said quickly, "Nah, forget it, you're busy with your story. You don't have time."

He looked so crestfallen that Keera had to smile.

"I can stay for a few minutes," Keera said.

"Cool," Jamar said happily. "See you in the studio."

When Keera entered the recording session, she felt like she had been transported into a hot, smoky club, like the ones she had read about but never been in. Jamar's music swirled around her, filling the studio. Jamar and his band were really good. Keera hadn't realized that Jamar could be serious about anything. But watching him play, she saw that he was as serious about his music as she was about everything else.

With his eyes closed, Jamar's handsome face was transfigured. She marveled at his strong hands, the same ones that had touched her so tenderly, slamming down hard, flying wildly over the keyboard. His close-cropped head bent to the rhythm. Caught up in the moment, he looked like someone else.

As if he could feel her thoughts, Jamar opened his eyes and stared straight at her. Losing his concentration for a split second, he let his fingers waver. The music faltered. The other instruments clattered out of sync and groaned to a halt. Rogue stopped singing.

"Hey, man, we were smoking. Pay attention to the gig," Rogue and the other band members complained.

"Be cool, Rogue. We'll just do it over," Jamar assured him.

Once again, he closed his eyes, and the music rose around him.

Not wanting to distract Jamar again, Keera made sure that the cameras were still taping. Then she slipped out. Neither she nor Jamar noticed Rogue's unhappy glance, which followed Keera out of the studio.

After a couple of hours of recording, the guys in Jamar's band broke for the day. Keera, working at the visual mixer in the control room, looked up as they passed by, pushing and shoving each other good-naturedly.

"Come on, man," they called to Jamar, who lingered in the doorway of the music control room.

"Go ahead, guys, I'll catch you later. I've got to mix in some special effects," Jamar shouted to them.

"Say, pretty Keera, nice to meet you," someone said on his way out.

"Bye," Keera answered shyly.

Rogue passed the main control room, gazing steadily at Keera through the glass portion of the wall, but not in a friendly way.

"So long, Keera. Don't tie our man down, little girl. He needs to be free and have fun," Rogue said warningly.

Startled, Keera was about to reply that she didn't have a clue as to what Rogue was talking about, when Jamar came out of the recording studio. Keera's gaze immediately shifted from Rogue to Jamar, who looked somewhere between exhausted and exhilarated. Distracted by Jamar, Keera forgot about Rogue's remark. By the time she remembered, Rogue was long gone.

"So, Keera, there's something I want to know," Jamar said, poking his head into the control room.

"Yes?" Keera asked.

"Did we do good?" Jamar asked eagerly, looking just like Keera's little brother after he hit a home run in Little League.

Keera's heart melted, seeing how much Jamar wanted her approval.

"You did good," Keera answered softly, her eyes smiling at Jamar.

Jamar's face glowed with pride. "Thanks. I was playing for you," he told her.

Keera could feel a red flush begin to creep up from below her throat.

Then Jamar took in a deep breath and moved closer to where Keera was sitting at the control panel. Clearing his throat, Jamar fidgeted awkwardly.

"Uh, Keera . . . about what happened at the beach," he began to say.

"At the beach . . ." Keera repeated cautiously, not knowing which way this was going to go.

"I'm really sorry I left you before the interview was over that day. It was immature and stupid, but . . ." Jamar took a deep breath and decided to just plunge right in. ". . . I guess I was so upset about what Moss was saying, and the way he was saying it—so flat and unemotional and all—well, I grew up playing in that lagoon, and, well . . ."

"Oh," Keera said. She immediately

understood. She'd been feeling a little funny about Mr. Moss's unemotional account as well. It was good to know that Jamar hadn't just run off on a whim.

But Keera was a little disappointed, too. She had been half hoping that Jamar would mention the few minutes *before* Moss showed up.

"So you're not mad?" Jamar asked anxiously.

"No, I'm not mad," Keera said slowly.

"Well, there's something else, too," Jamar began.

Keera just waited, looking down at the floor, too nervous to meet Jamar's eyes.

Watching Keera and getting no encouragement from her, Jamar felt his confidence begin to falter. His palms were all sweaty. The words, which usually fell out of his mouth, weren't there. Maybe he'd just dreamed something was going on between them at the beach. Maybe she really was still mad about his leaving.

Keera waited for Jamar to say something. But it was the sharp ring of the telephone on Jamar's desk that broke the silence.

Jamar went over and picked it up. His bright smile faded quickly as he listened. He sank down into his chair, and his expression changed from dismay to worry to anger so fast, Keera felt like she was eavesdropping just watching his face through the glass.

Jamar turned away from Keera slightly, mumbled something into the phone, and listened a few minutes longer. Then he slammed down the phone and noisily pushed back his chair. He ran his hand over the top of his head and down the back of his neck, then sat motionless in his chair, looking as if he might cry.

"Is everything okay?" Keera asked with concern, moving to stand in the doorway of the control room.

"No," Jamar answered.

"What's wrong, Jamar?" Keera asked gently, coming closer.

"That was my mom," Jamar began slowly. "It's been just the two of us for so long, and now . . . " Jamar broke off. "I gotta go," he said suddenly. "Catch you later," Jamar called as he raced out of the station.

From the window, Keera could see Jamar pedaling his bike as fast as it would go. He hadn't even bothered to plug in his headset.

Keera wondered if she and Jamar would ever get together.

As he sped for home Jamar was wondering the very same thing.

Chapter Seven

*A*fter Jamar left the studio, Keera tried to concentrate on her story. But she couldn't get the worried look on Jamar's face out of her mind.

Then Amanda rushed into the station, looking for Drew.

"He hasn't been around all day," Keera commented. "Why, what's up?"

"Oh, Drew knew that I wanted to go over my intro with him. He told me that he was free most of today, so I rushed over as soon as I finished it. Now he's not even here!" Amanda complained.

"Trouble in paradise?" Keera quipped.

"Of course not. Something else really important must have come up," Amanda said.

"Well, I was just going to quit for the day. And I was thinking about getting something to eat . . ." Keera said.

"Hey, cool. Let's eat at the Snack Shack. I haven't been there since school let out."

A few minutes later, Amanda and Keera pulled up to the Shack in Amanda's car. Everyone inside seemed to know Amanda, waving and calling her name. Nobody even noticed Keera.

After ordering her usual double-chili cheeseburger and atomic fries from a retro-looking waitress with a close-cut, faintly purple bob, Amanda sipped her triple-thick chocolate milkshake.

Keera, drinking a diet Sprite and waiting for her salad, just shook her head in amazement.

"Keera, what?" Amanda asked, laughing.

"It's you," Keera said. "Here you are, looking like something from a magazine cover, ordering a burger, fries, and a shake. If I ate like that, I'd have wall-to-wall pimples, and I'd be the size of a recreational vehicle."

"I know. My other friends say the same thing. I guess that's one thing I'm lucky about. I can always eat whatever I want," Amanda said, cheerfully digging into the food the waitress placed before her.

"Do you come here a lot?" Keera asked, picking at her salad. Keera didn't hang out at the Shack. It was pricier than most of the diners, and it was too far to get to from school unless you had a car. Keera usually brought a snack to school, and she walked home to study as soon as school was done.

"All the time, during school," Amanda told her between bites. "You know, the whole crowd hangs out here, Samantha, Tyler . . . although I don't think I'll be hanging out with Tyler Scott any time soon," Amanda said decisively.

"You mean Tyler Scott of Scott Enterprises?" Keera asked, remembering the name from her interview with Mr. Moss.

"One and the same," Amanda answered. "Did Jamar or Hero mention what happened at the football field the other day?"

Keera shook her head no.

"Good. Then maybe they didn't think it was such a big deal. But I was furious," Amanda said, tossing her hair back.

"What happened?" Keera asked.

"Hero and Jamar came to football practice to interview the team. While Hero was talking to the starting players, Tyler was as rude to Hero as I've ever seen him be to anyone," Amanda said. Just talking about it made her angry all over again.

"What did Hero do?" Keera asked.

"He got angrier than I've ever seen anyone get. I think he would have punched Tyler's lights out, but Jamar stopped him. I know nothing I could say would have stopped him," Amanda added, remembering how Hero had turned angrily on her.

Then, with a glance at Keera, Amanda continued, "I think Jamar is a great guy."

"Yeah, he seems really nice," Keera agreed noncommittally. She wasn't quite ready to admit anything more yet.

Quickly changing the subject, Keera said, "I think Hero is really great, too."

"He's okay. Kind of moody and sarcastic, though. Still, he is very cute," Amanda said, remembering how good he had looked the other day at the field.

"But he's definitely not my type, like Drew is," Amanda added quickly. "If it weren't for working at KSS, I'm sure we'd never even have spoken to each other."

"Well, just think, if you and I hadn't decided to work at KSS this summer, we probably would have gone through high school without ever knowing each other," Keera pointed out.

"Hey, I told you the first day I knew who you were," Amanda said. "Everyone knows you, Keera. You're the smartest girl in the school—'the girl most destined for success,'" Amanda told her, quoting someone in a pinched, nasal voice.

Keera's skin flushed dark red and she looked at Amanda in amazement. "Everyone knows me? You mean, everyone knows *you*, Amanda. Everywhere you go, people

90

wave and say hello. I don't talk to anyone except my best friend, Jeanette, and a couple of other friends," Keera protested.

"Sure, but the teachers all know you, and they always hold you up as an example when they want to make a point," Amanda told her.

"They do?" Keera asked. She was astonished. It never occurred to her that anyone other than her friends at school knew she was alive.

"Absolutely. And we'd all groan inside whenever we heard your name, because we knew it meant we had 'fallen short of the mark,'" Amanda mimicked another teacher's voice.

"Great, so everyone hates me," Keera said self-consciously.

"Definitely not," Amanda said emphatically. "It's the teachers we can't stand. Besides, you're not anything like the way I thought you'd be. You know, you're not up-in-the-clouds, or condescending, or anything like that."

"Thanks," Keera said. "You're not at all the way I thought you'd be, either," she admitted to Amanda.

Now it was Amanda's turn to look surprised. "What do you mean?" she asked.

"Well, you know," Keera began, "even

though you're the prettiest, most popular girl in Cliffside High, you're really nice, and not the stuck-up snob I always thought you were."

"Thanks a lot," Amanda said. A little smile played around the edges of her mouth.

Keera continued, "No, really. When I found out you were working at KSS, I couldn't believe it. I didn't think girls like you worked during the summer. I would have thought you'd be off having fun, sailing or water skiing, like your friends."

"Well, I'm not, am I?" Amanda said defiantly.

"No. But I've been wondering—how come?" Keera asked timidly, afraid that she had offended Amanda.

Amanda thought for a moment before she spoke.

"To tell you the truth, I'm kind of tired of always doing the same thing with the same crowd," Amanda told her. "I mean, I've known them all forever. And, for as long as I can remember, they've spent half their time doing or saying mean things about each other. The other half, they're being mean about someone else. It's boring, and a lot like my parents' lives. I wanted to do something different. When Mr. Fredericks told me about this job, I thought it might be fun to work on my own television show. And it's been great, meeting you guys, and talking about stuff that's really interesting. And then, of course, there's Drew . . ." Amanda trailed off, sighing.

"Why the big sigh?" Keera asked, genuinely puzzled.

"Oh, it's this thing with Drew," Amanda confided, tracing her finger around the bottom of her empty shake glass.

"What do you mean?" Keera asked.

"Well, he's such a wonderful man. He's warm, gentle, supportive, sincere. And he listens to me—I mean really listens. I feel like we share all these secret understandings. I know what he's going to say before he says it, and he's the same way with me. When I'm with him, it's like no one else in the world matters." Amanda hesitated. "Are you really sure you want to hear all this?"

"Of course," Keera said, smiling. "What are friends for?"

Flashing her a grateful look, Amanda continued, "Well, it's just that I think I'm totally in love with Drew, which is ridiculous. I mean, I've only known him for a week, but I can't stop thinking about him. I know he's a little older, but it just feels so right to me . . ." Amanda faltered, as if afraid to say what came next.

" . . . but you're not sure if he feels the same way about you?" Keera finished Amanda's sentence.

Amanda's eyes filled, her lips trembled. Unable to speak, she nodded her head.

"I know just how you feel," Keera sympathized.

"You do?"

"Uh-huh," Keera said. Should she tell Amanda about her feelings for Jamar?

Just then, Keera glanced out the front window of the Snack Shack and noticed a familiar figure sauntering down the street.

It was Jamar. Keera was about to wave to him and motion for him to come in, when she realized that Jamar wasn't walking by himself. And he wasn't walking with his friends. He was walking with his arm around another girl. A pretty little thing with a short, tight skirt and a tiny, fitted top.

Chapter Eight

Keera's face went numb. Her stomach churned viciously, and she thought she might throw up. She kept nodding woodenly at Amanda, who was asking her what was wrong. The words Rogue had spoken to her at the studio rang in her ears, "Don't tie our man down." What a joke, Keera thought to herself.

Following Keera's gaze, Amanda was surprised to see Jamar with his arm around some girl. Before this moment, Amanda had been sure that Jamar was interested in Keera. Judging from Keera's reaction, Amanda thought, it was pretty clear that Keera had fallen for Jamar, too.

"Come on, Keera, let's blow this popsicle stand," Amanda said softly, motioning the waitress for the check. Then she gently guided Keera out of the Snack Shack.

Keera's eyes were blurry with tears. She tried telling Amanda she would make the long walk home by herself, but somehow her lips couldn't quite form the words.

"Hey, I've got an idea," Amanda said. "Let's have a cat party."

Keera blinked her eyes to clear the tears. "What did you say?"

"You know, a sleepover. Just you and me. We'll stop at the video store on the way to your house to pick up your clothes, and we'll pop popcorn, watch movies, paint our toenails, and talk all night long. I haven't had a sleepover since I was twelve. Won't it be great?" Amanda asked excitedly.

"I guess so," Keera said slowly, coming out of her trance and trying to put Jamar out of her mind.

"Well, you could be a little more enthusiastic," Amanda said with mock annoyance.

"I still have a ton of work to do on the visual mixer . . ." Keera began.

"I have a plan," Amanda said. "You come home with me and help me put together the outfits I'm going to tape, and I'll help you mix your footage after the weekend. I'm a real pro at it, now, just like Drew said I would be," Amanda told her proudly. "It's all settled." Seeing how upset Keera was, Amanda wasn't about to take "no" for an answer.

Drawing a shaky breath, Keera said with

a small smile, "I'd love to, Amanda, really. I haven't had a sleepover since . . . I don't remember."

Amanda hugged Keera sympathetically. She knew how bad Keera must feel. If Amanda had ever seen Drew with someone else, she'd want to die. As quickly as the thought had come, Amanda dismissed it from her mind. That just wasn't possible.

Riding together in the car, Keera was grateful that the wind whipping around their heads prevented further conversation. Maybe she would tell Amanda how she felt about Jamar, later, after they'd seen a few movies.

Amanda glanced at Keera to see how she was doing. She's so different from Samantha, Amanda thought to herself. Samantha would be complaining nonstop if she'd seen someone she liked with another girl, or else she'd start eyeing the next guy who walked down the street. Maybe Keera is in love with Jamar the way I'm in love with Drew, Amanda thought.

Amanda imagined driving somewhere with Drew, maybe to Cliffside Bluff for a picnic. The ocean waves crashed below them, the sun was warm on their faces. Amanda could almost feel Drew's warm breath hovering above her face as he bent his head closer and closer, until their lips almost touched.

"Amanda, my house is over there," Keera pointed.

Amanda quickly swerved over to the curb, pulling up in front of Keera's house.

Keera jumped out. "I'll just be a minute," she said, not especially wanting Amanda to come in. She didn't know what condition the house would be in, but if her parents and younger brother had left it in its usual state of confusion, then crayons, papers, clothes, and toys would be strewn everywhere. Keera certainly didn't want Amanda to see it that way.

Just as Keera had thought, her parents were out with her brother, and the house was a mess. Leaving them a note with Amanda's name and phone number, Keera quickly stuffed some things in an overnight bag and ran back out to the car.

Amanda and Keera gave each other a quick smile.

"Ready?" Amanda asked.

"Absolutely," Keera answered.

When Amanda and Keera entered Amanda's house, Keera tried not to gape at the mansion that Amanda called home. Her head twisted up, down, and around, taking in the twenty-foot-high, ornately decorated ceilings, the marble floors, the twinkling chandeliers.

Keera was glad that she hadn't invited Amanda in to her house. What would Amanda have thought, comparing Keera's house to this? What must she already think? Keera wondered, thinking of her street filled with row houses, a sorry contrast to the development of manor-like houses where Amanda lived in Cliffside Heights.

Amanda breezed up the wide, curving stairway, leading Keera through the house to her room on the second floor. Amanda called hello to her mother, who was in her palatial bedroom on the other side of the stairwell, getting dressed for dinner.

"Amanda, you're home early," Mrs. Townsend called from her dressing room.

"She's so observant, isn't she?" Amanda whispered to Keera, who tried not to giggle nervously.

"Amanda, would you come here for a minute? I want to know what you think of this dress for tonight," Mrs. Townsend asked.

"Uh, I've got a friend over, Mom," Amanda started to say.

"Oh, is Samantha here? What a nice surprise!" Mrs. Townsend said, coming to the doorway of her room. She was dressed in a royal blue silk strapless gown, with a sapphire choker at her throat and sapphire studs glittering beneath her upswept blonde hair.

"Oh, hello," Mrs. Townsend said, raising her eyebrow ever so slightly. "I don't believe we've met," she added formally.

"Mom, this is Keera Johnson. Remember I told you about the new kids I met at the KSS station?" Amanda reminded her. "Keera works at KSS, too."

"Hi, Mrs. Townsend. It's nice to meet you," Keera said in a small voice.

"And you, Keera," Mrs. Townsend replied, taking in Keera's appearance with a not-so-subtle glance.

"Well, I've got to be going. I'm meeting your father and a client of his at the Club for dinner this evening," Mrs. Townsend told Amanda. "I was going to leave you a note and tell you to order in something if you want. It's Consuela's weekend off. Will you be able to manage dinner on your own tonight?"

"Yes, Mother. I think I can handle take-out," Amanda said, rolling her eyes. Keera suppressed an anxious giggle.

"Well, I'm off. How do I look?" Mrs. Townsend asked Amanda.

"I think you look wonderful, Mrs. Townsend," Keera blurted out.

Amanda looked quizzically at Keera.

"You look nice, Mom," Amanda answered in a flat tone.

"Thank you, girls." Mrs. Townsend smiled graciously. Then she glided down the massive stairway and out the front door.

When the door closed behind Mrs. Townsend, Keera was finally able to exhale. She had never met anyone quite like Mrs. Townsend before. It had never occurred to Keera that there were mothers who dressed like movie stars and who ordered takeout instead of making dinner for you when you got home.

"Bye, Mom, have a nice time," Amanda called down to the closed door.

Keera looked at Amanda questioningly.

"Your mother is beautiful, Amanda. She looks just like you," Keera told her.

Amanda shrugged. She didn't want to talk about her mother right now.

"Let's put these videos down, order a pizza, and make scads of popcorn," Amanda said with an impish grin. "Then we can change into sleep tees, and, after we eat, we can start putting together the outfits. You should see some of the stuff I've collected."

The girls donned their pajama shirts and, with huge bowls of buttered popcorn in their laps, settled comfortably on the floor of Amanda's luxurious bedroom, in front of the TV, waiting for their pizza to arrive.

From the corner of her eye, Keera looked at Amanda. With her hair piled on top of her head in a ponytail, dressed in her extra-large Cliffside High T-shirt, Amanda seemed about twelve. She certainly didn't look like the perfectly dressed Amanda Townsend of high school fame.

Keera looked around at Amanda's bedroom in awe. Amanda had state-of-the-art everything: television, CD player, VCR, computer, and stuff Keera hadn't ever seen before. The walls were covered in coffee-cream-colored paper; thick, ivory carpeting covered the floor. Amanda's bed was king-sized, piled high with creamy spreads and ruffled lace and satin pillows. Original oil paintings and prints decorated the walls of the room, providing the only splashes of color.

Everything looked perfect and nothing was out of place. Mentally comparing Amanda's room to her own, Keera thought of the jumble of clothes, books, and tapes that filled up her small bedroom, which she and her father had painted all by themselves, and the worn area rug that covered the bare wooden floor. Posters and pictures decorated her walls, hung at all different angles.

"Gee, Amanda, this room is perfect," Keera sighed.

"It's nice," Amanda said agreeably. Then she added wistfully, "It's a lot different from my old bedroom in our last house. I loved that old house. It had secret stairwells and a great big attic. My room was under the eaves, and it had everything: my posters, my pictures, an old vanity with all my mother's leftover makeup and perfumes, my grand mother's trunk with all my dress-up clothes, even my old stuffed animals.

"But when we moved into this mausoleum last year, my mother decided it was out with the old and in with the new. She was determined to create the perfect house. My room is from *Architectural Digest*, Volume 29, Issue 33, Page 54," Amanda added, imitating her mother's voice perfectly.

"But if you like this room, you ought to see Kit's room," Amanda said with a grin.

"Who's Kit?" Keera asked.

Leaving the popcorn bowls in front of the television, the girls walked down the wide marble hallway.

"Kit's my younger sister. Lucky for us,

103

she's away at sleepaway camp for the summer, so the house is essentially pest-free," Amanda explained, leading the way.

"Here we are. Take a peek," Amanda said with a flourish.

Keera peered inside Kit's room. It looked like every little girl's fantasy: pink canopy bed, pastel carpeting, antique white-painted dresser on claw feet, and a matching rocking chair on which several hand-painted porcelain dolls sat primly, dressed in velvet, brocade, and silk. Cases of doll collections adorned the walls, and delicately hand-stenciled wallpaper with sprigs of flowers floated behind the glass cabinets.

Again, Keera couldn't help comparing Amanda's little sister's room to the one her brothers shared. There was nothing perfect about their piles of clothes and sneakers, the raggedy basketball hoop on the door, the Michael Jordan posters everywhere. But, somehow, their room looked like them—casual and comfortable. Kit's and Amanda's rooms looked like . . . museums.

"Wow," Keera said. "Kit's room looks like something out of a magazine, too."

"No, this one my mother thought of all by herself. She'd always wanted a room like this when she was thirteen. So now Kit has it. Of course, Kit is a total tomboy, so you can imagine how much she likes her room," Amanda said. "But Mother's happy, and as Dad always says, 'That's what counts.'"

Keera didn't know what to say. It was stupid to feel sorry for Amanda, with all her money and beautiful things. But she did, just a little, anyway.

The chiming of the doorbell interrupted Keera's thoughts.

"Pizza!" both girls shouted simultaneously.

"Beat you down the stairs," Amanda called, racing away with Keera close behind her.

Giggling and breathless, Amanda flung open the door. But instead of the pizza delivery boy, Samantha Walker stood there. Her curly blonde hair formed a misty cloud around her chubby, but pretty, face. Her peach-colored silk T-shirt fit a little too snugly across her chest, and her designer jeans dug in just a little at her rounded waist.

"Hi, Amanda," Samantha said.

"Hey, Samantha," Amanda said, catching her breath. "We thought you were the pizza guy."

Looking curiously at Keera, Samantha said, "Oh, hello."

"Samantha, this is Keera Johnson. She works with me at KSS," Amanda said.

Samantha nodded her head slightly. Then she looked Amanda and Keera up and down, wrinkling her nose at what she saw.

"You girls look like you're dressed for a night in," Samantha said. "I thought we could go cruising down Main Street, Amanda, and maybe get something to eat at the Shack."

Carefully waiting a full minute, Samantha turned to Keera and said, "Of course, you're invited to come, too."

Keera held her breath, waiting to hear Amanda's reply. After all, Samantha was Amanda's best friend. Driving down Main Street probably sounded more exciting to Amanda than watching movies and eating pizza and popcorn and working on the fashion outfits.

Without skipping a beat, Amanda replied firmly, "No, thanks, Samantha. We're having a kind of combination slumber party and working dinner. You're invited to stay and party with us for awhile," she added politely.

"Sure, that would be great," Keera said, hoping Samantha would turn them down.

Samantha looked them over once more. "I don't think so, Amanda," Samantha sniffed. "I was expecting to run into Tyler and some of the other kids and maybe drive down to the beach." She fluffed her hair out.

"So I guess that's a big no?" Amanda said.

"Maybe we can do something tomorrow night, Amanda. If you don't have other plans," Samantha said, pointedly looking at Keera.

Exchanging a secret glance with Keera, Amanda said, "I'll have to see how much work we get done tonight, Samantha. You know, our show airs on the Fourth, and we've still got tons to do." Then, seeing the dissatisfied expression on Samantha's face, Amanda added quickly, "But I'll give you a call, I promise."

"Oh, Amanda. Ever since you took this television job, you haven't been any fun. You don't come water skiing or sailing with us during the day, and now you're working nights, too! It's summer, Amanda. We're supposed to be having a good time!" Samantha whined.

"Look, Samantha, Keera and I have to get this stuff done. But you go have a nice time. I'll call you tomorrow and you can tell me about tonight. Okay?"

"Okay, fine. I guess I'll talk to you tomorrow, then," Samantha said. "Uh—nice to meet you . . . Keera," Samantha added, sounding like it was anything but.

Then, turning abruptly on her elevated

heels, Samantha tripped off toward her bright red Camaro, nearly knocking down the pizza delivery guy, who had just ridden up on his motorcycle.

Amanda invited the pizza delivery guy in and pointed him in the direction of the kitchen. Then she closed the door and sank against it, sighing.

Keera watched Amanda for a cue. Was Amanda unhappy that she'd invited her over? Had she really wanted to go out with Samantha?

Amanda smiled widely at Keera. "Come on, I can hear that pizza calling my name," Amanda said with absolutely no trace of regret.

Keera grinned back.

As Samantha was about to get into her Camaro, Tyler Scott drove up in his father's latest Ferrari.

"Hey, Tyler," Samantha called.

"Hi, Samantha," Tyler said. "I see Amanda's home."

Samantha fumed. Why didn't Tyler ever notice her? Why was he always thinking about Amanda?

"Well, good luck trying to budge her," Samantha called, yanking open her car door.

"That's why I 'borrowed' Dad's Ferrari," Tyler said smugly. "I thought she'd like to take it for a little ride around Cliffside."

Samantha would have loved to go riding in Tyler's Ferrari, so she couldn't help taunting him.

"Oh, I wouldn't count on that, Tyler. Amanda's very busy 'working' with her new KSS friend right now, and she doesn't have time for us anymore," Samantha said. Then Samantha sidled over to Tyler. "But I'd like to take a ride in the Ferrari," she said softly.

"Maybe some other time," Tyler said distractedly, as the lights went on in Amanda's room.

"Great!" Samantha said sarcastically. She walked to her car and flung herself behind the wheel, then drove off in a cloud of smoke.

It was then that Tyler noticed the motorcycle parked in the driveway. Seeing the lights in Amanda's room, Tyler tried to figure out what was going on.

Who was this KSS friend who was working late with Amanda on a Friday night? Eyeing the motorcycle suspiciously, Tyler was thunderstruck. Could Hero Montoya be the KSS friend Samantha was talking about?

Maybe that's why Amanda got so hostile the other day when I put Hero in his place, Tyler thought angrily. There *is* something going on between them!

Well, Tyler wasn't going to make a fool of himself, calling for Amanda when she was obviously entertaining Hero in her room. Tyler's eyes narrowed to slits. He could just imagine what was going on between them. The thought of Amanda snuggling up to Hero was more than Tyler could bear.

Angrily, Tyler threw himself back into his father's Ferrari. He was going to have to do something about this situation. Tyler Scott wasn't about to lose Amanda Townsend to anyone, much less to someone like Hero Montoya.

Chapter Nine

The following week, Hero, Amanda, and Keera were glued to the monitors in the main control room, editing their segments. The door slammed open and Jamar rushed in, bringing a gust of warm air with him.

Keera's heart did a little leap when Jamar entered. She hadn't seen Jamar since last Friday, and that had been just fine with Keera. After talking the whole thing over with Amanda, Keera had decided that the best thing to do about Jamar was to move on. She would keep their relationship cool and professional, distant and calm. She would *not* let her emotions get out of control when he was around.

Keera gave him a distracted wave and went back to her work.

Amanda smiled briefly. "Great music for the 'Hot Shots' segment, Jamar. Thanks," Amanda told him.

"Yeah, sure," Jamar told her. He looked expectantly at Keera, wanting to know what she thought of the backgrounds for her spot.

"The music you did for mine was very good, too, Jamar," Keera said stiffly. Then she went back to her monitor, as if Jamar was nothing but a pencil holder on a distant desk.

Any other day, Jamar would have commented on the less than enthusiastic response. But today, he was wiped. He'd been walking and talking for days, and he'd been working on Amanda's and Keera's background music in between. He still had Hero's background music to score.

"You're late, bro," Hero remarked calmly, not taking his eyes from his monitor.

"I've been busy," Jamar said, rubbing his hands over his face.

Yeah, busy with your little girlfriend, Keera thought.

"Want to talk about it?" Hero asked.

Jamar ran his hands over his face again, harder, scrunching his cheeks. He closed his eyes, looking like he was either going to fall asleep or cry. "Nah, man, I've got too much stuff to do, including working on your piece," he said.

"Come on, Jamar. Let's get some coffee first. You look like you need it, and you won't be much good to me if you can't see straight," Hero insisted. He took Jamar's arm and led him out the door.

Jamar turned back to wave at Keera, who was stonily staring at a monitor.

What's with her? Jamar wondered.

But then Jamar's more immediate problems took over his thoughts, as Hero guided Jamar over to his Harley and they rode off toward a nearby coffee shop.

With a cup of steaming coffee sitting before him, Jamar slumped down in his seat, resting his heavy head on his hands.

"So, what's up, dude?" Hero asked.

"It's Jolie," Jamar began.

Hero raised his eyebrows. "Girl trouble?" he asked.

"Not the kind you think," Jamar explained. "Jolie's my half sister. She's only fourteen, but you'd think she was twenty-one the way she dresses and talks. Anyway, she just came back last week to live with us for the summer. She's been living up North with her father, where she's been going to a fancy private school."

"So far, I don't see the prob," Hero said. "I mean, I guess younger sisters can be a pain, but if it's only a part-time thing, what's the big deal?"

"Well, last Friday she ran away. My mother called me at work, hysterical, to say that Jolie had taken her things and left. They had a fight about her clothes, her makeup, her music—

everything. Jolie said she was sleeping anywhere but our house, and she split. I had to race out of the studio like a fool . . . " Jamar stopped, remembering that he had been about to ask Keera out when he had to leave. Judging from Keera's cool behavior and her non-existent greeting, Jamar was sure he'd blown his chances with her for good. That thought was so depressing, it made his head feel even heavier.

"I found Jolie at the bus station, begging for bus fare," Jamar continued. "I had to walk around town with her for the rest of the day and half the night, trying to convince her to come home, telling her that our mom just wasn't used to having her around, looking all grown-up and . . . sexy." Jamar took a big gulp of his coffee.

"How sexy could a fourteen-year-old look?" Hero wanted to know.

"Sexier than she should," Jamar said, smiling for the first time that morning.

"So, did you convince her?" Hero asked, glad that he'd been able to make Jamar crack a smile.

"Yeah, she finally broke down and said she'd come home. But then I spent most of the weekend trying to get Jolie and my mom to work it out. Man, those women can cry. I hate when chicks cry. I never know what to do," Jamar told Hero.

Thinking about his mother's tears, Hero nodded. "I know what you mean."

"You do?" Jamar asked.

"Sure." Hero spoke haltingly. "I mean, I don't have any sisters, but my parents are . . . well, they don't get along too well anymore, and my mother cries a lot. I never know what to say to her, or if I should even say anything." Taking a deep breath, Hero admitted, "I feel really bad for my dad, too."

"Sounds like a bad scene," Jamar said consolingly.

"Yeah, my parents have made a real mess out of their marriage. I guess I'm not too good at relationships, myself," Hero admitted, thinking of Amanda.

"Me either," Jamar confided. "You know, last week, when Keera and I were taping her lagoon scene, I thought we had really started cooking. There was definitely electricity in the air. Then that jerk, Moss, showed up for his interview, and it was downhill from there.

"Then, last Friday, I had actually gotten it together to ask Keera out. I've wanted to do that since we started working, and this was the first day I finally got up the courage. And I'm pretty sure she would have said yes. But then I got the call from my mother—and now, the way Keera's been acting, it seems like that day at the beach is light-years away."

"Hey, I didn't know you were so serious about Keera." Hero lightly poked Jamar in the side.

Jamar lowered his eyes, "Yeah, well . . ."

"Aw, Keera's the type who'd understand about your sister. She's just a perfectionist, and she's worried about the deadline," Hero assured Jamar.

"What about you and Amanda?" Jamar asked boldly.

"What do you mean?" Hero responded. A wary look crept over his face.

"Aw, come on, Hero. Don't play with me. I just spilled my guts to you. Besides, anyone with half a brain can see that you've got it bad for Amanda," Jamar teased.

"Well, in case you hadn't noticed, Amanda's got her heart set on our fearless leader, Drew," Hero said with a shrug. Then, looking at his watch, Hero changed the subject.

"Come on, man. Let's get back to the grind. I want to show you how I changed my piece, and you need to come up with the background music—fast," Hero reminded him.

When Hero and Jamar returned to the

studio, Amanda and Keera were closeted with Drew in his office. The guys went into the screening room so that Hero could show Jamar his final cut.

Instead of doing a straight Cliffside sports retrospective, Hero had decided to put a little spin on the show, calling it "Great Moments and the Flip Side." He'd put together a montage of clips from the last ten years of Cliffside High's football games, showing the winning touchdowns, the unbelievable passes, the running records, and other great moments. Hero also used some of the footage that Jamar had shot of this year's Cliffside team on the opening day of practice, to show that Cliffside was preparing for the new season.

Then he showed the flip side—some of the outtakes of local footage that Drew had at the station, featuring embarrassing mistakes and bad plays.

"And the star, at his very own request, is none other than our good friend, Tyler Scott," Hero added, grinning widely.

Jamar hooted as he watched some of Tyler's funnier moments.

"I've got just the music for this. Let's get to work," Jamar told Hero excitedly. For the moment he forgot all about Jolie, his mother—and even Keera.

117

Chapter Ten

*I*t was D-day minus one, and counting. The four KSS-TV staffers had gone over their segments a zillion times, making sure that the pieces were all in sync and running smoothly. Today, for the first time, the four were going to run the show in its entirety for Drew, and for each other. Everyone was a little on edge. They milled about, waiting for Drew to get off the phone so they could all go into the screening room.

As everyone waited anxiously, Amanda grew dreamy-eyed thinking about Drew and how it would be if they were together. After almost two weeks of working closely with him, Amanda felt she knew Drew better than anyone she'd ever met in her life. She adored the way his eyes danced when he laughed at her quips. When Amanda spoke, Drew listened, making Amanda feel as though she were the most important person in the world.

Amanda could hardly wait for tomorrow's Beach Bash. Drew had promised to meet them all to celebrate their television debut. Closing her eyes, Amanda imagined herself drifting in Drew's arms as they danced on the beach. The misty air would wash over them like a cool shower. Drew would bring her close, closer, until her body melted into his. His lips would touch hers, gently at first, then more hungrily. Amanda could feel her fingers curling around the tendrils of hair that grew along the back of Drew's neck . . .

Suddenly Amanda felt someone touch her shoulder. Thinking it was Drew, Amanda looked up adoringly. She was startled to see Hero's face peering down at her.

"Hey, Amanda," Hero said, taken aback by the soft, dreamy look in her eyes. "Drew's ready for us in the viewing room."

Amanda jumped up quickly. "Oh, great. Let's go."

Hero followed Amanda into the viewing room, where Drew, Keera, and Jamar were waiting. Keera had taken care to sit on the opposite side of the room from Jamar. Amanda immediately sought out the seat next to Drew. He smiled welcomingly at her as she settled down beside him.

At the sight of Drew and Amanda, Hero's heart sank. After what had happened on the football field, Hero figured Amanda wouldn't ever be interested in him. What a wimp he must seem like in comparison to self-confident Drew, Hero thought unhappily.

Then the lights went dark, the show intro came on, and Amanda, Hero, Keera, and Jamar sat spellbound. They were on the air!

Amanda's "Hot Shots" segment came first. Everyone howled at all the right moments, and even Hero laughed. Jamar whistled and cheered when Amanda and Keera modeled the top ten "most ridiculous" looks of summer.

Drew gave Amanda a quick hug, and Amanda's heart thumped so loudly, she thought everyone would hear. Then Drew whispered, "We need to talk after the screening. Come see me in my office."

Amanda flushed. Maybe it was finally going to happen. Drew was going to tell her how much he loved her. He would say that they had to be together, always. Amanda would have to be the one to stand back, lovingly, but in control, keeping Drew from crushing her to him, bringing some sense to their madness.

As she glanced sideways at Drew, Amanda's pulse quickened. She imagined herself tracing the outline of Drew's full lips with her finger.

Keera's segment, "Operation Cliffside," came on the screen. The room grew very quiet as the camera panned the cordoned-off lagoon where local manufacturers had illegally dumped toxic wastes. It was impossible not to feel pangs of guilt, sadness, and anger when the camera focused on the dead fish, the sick-looking birds, and the black, oily spots on the sand.

Keera had decided to use her own voice and that of Mr. Moss as a voiceover, keeping the camera focused only on the beach. Jamar had scored the music so that when Keera showed the good part of the beach, the music was upbeat with bird and surf noises intermingled. But when Keera panned the closed-down lagoon and shoreline, the viewers would hear only silence—as if to illustrate the absence of life.

Sensitive to the distinction, Amanda shivered. Hero bent his head. Jamar and Keera stared straight ahead, knowing every angle and twist by heart.

Drew stopped the tape for a moment.

Keera held her breath. She just knew he was going to tell her that it was too hard-hitting, maybe even too dull. Drew turned around, staring hard at Keera for a moment.

"Keera, I just want you to know I think that was a first-class piece of journalism—

on any level. It's something to proud of," Drew said seriously.

Everyone murmured their agreement. For a millisecond, Amanda's pride was a little tweaked. But she was too happy for Keera, and too impressed by Keera's piece, to feel out of joint for long.

Keera blushed furiously.

"Thanks. But some of the credit goes to Jamar," Keera added, glancing sideways at him. "The score really makes the whole point."

Looking hopefully over at Keera, Jamar smiled tentatively. But he was quick to say, "No way, girl, that gig was all you."

Keera looked down, staring at a spot on the rug, not knowing what to say next.

Without waiting for any other comments, Drew snapped off the lights, again plunging the room into darkness.

Next up was Jamar's "Jammin'" segment. The room was filled with the sights and sounds of Jamar's band. It was like being in the middle of a great big party.

Amanda and Keera wriggled in their seats, while Drew tapped his knee and his head bobbed up and down with the rhythm. Hero's eyes sparkled in the dark. His body tensed, wanting to let loose and dance, but something held him back. Hero didn't want to look like a fool again in front of Amanda.

Jamar just watched himself on the screen, looking for all the world like a little boy who waited up for Santa—and actually got to see him.

When Jamar's segment ended, Hero drew in his breath nervously. He wiped his palms along the sides of his jeans. Anxiously running his hand through that front lock of hair, he waited for his segment to kick in.

As the tape rolled, Hero was afraid to watch Amanda's face. He had told only Jamar about the new "Flip Side" ending featuring Tyler. Hero wasn't sure just how friendly Amanda and Tyler really were. In just about five minutes, they'd all find out.

As the bloopers rolled, some in fast forward, some in slow-mo, with Jamar's take on Charlie Chaplin music in the background, Amanda and Keera started to giggle.

Jamar and Drew laughed right out loud.

When the lights came back up, Drew came over and slapped Hero enthusiastically on the back.

"Good work, Hero. You balanced out the tribute and the funny stuff perfectly," Drew told him, pulling out the final tape.

Then he turned to all four of them, looking serious.

"First, I want you all to know that I think you've done a terrific job. It all looks very professionally done, and, what's more, you did it all by yourselves. There is one thing I want you to know. We do have a number of private donors who contribute to the running of this station. Local businesses and stuff. It's very possible that after your show runs— especially your segment, Keera—we'll end up taking some heat from these people. But that's what honest programming is about. Anyway, that's my job and my worry, not yours. I just thought it was important that you know it," Drew told them solemnly. Then he smiled. "Right now, you can all consider yourselves professional TV producers."

Then he left the room to store the tape in the final cuts drawer, which he kept locked in his office.

Hero's eyes gleamed proudly. He could see Amanda was feeling proud of herself, too. Their eyes met and locked for a moment. Then Amanda smiled so brilliantly at Hero, he was taken aback. It was the first time her attention hadn't left the room when Drew did. Hero's hopes for getting together with Amanda started to blossom all over again.

"Your segment was really good, Hero. I loved the part where the quarterback throws the ball backward and the other team picks it up and races like mad for a touchdown. I remember when it happened, and we all felt like crying. But the way you handled it, we can all laugh at the memory—not to mention laughing at the quarterback, too!"

"Thanks, Amanda. I think your piece came out great, too," Hero said, giving her a shy smile.

Amanda was caught off guard again by how handsome Hero looked when he was smiling. It was nothing like how threatening he could appear when he was angry, Amanda thought, remembering the scene with Tyler.

Keera came over and gave Hero a quick hug. "Your segment was great," Keera let him know.

"Yours, too," Hero told her.

Forgetting herself, Keera turned to Jamar, ready to share her enthusiasm with him. Surprised by her smile, Jamar started toward her.

Abruptly, Keera remembered that she didn't want anything to do with him. The smile froze on her lips.

"Hey, everybody. I've got a plan. Let's go out and celebrate our first television hour," Jamar said.

126

"Uh, I'll have to pass," Keera said quickly. For the first time, Keera noticed how Jamar's cheeks dimpled in the corners when he smiled really wide. Hardening her heart, she sidled past Jamar and scurried from the room. "See you tomorrow at the Bash," she called over her shoulder.

"Hey, Keera, wait up," Jamar said, hurrying out after her.

Amanda sighed tragically at the sight of Keera and the forlorn-looking Jamar. Such a shame, these star-crossed lovers, Amanda thought. Then she held her arms together, shivering a bit at the memory of Drew's whispered "We have to talk."

Hero broke into Amanda's thoughts. "Guess that leaves just you and me to celebrate," he said huskily, his hopes getting the better of him.

It took Amanda a moment to understand what Hero was talking about.

"Oh, yeah, thanks, Hero. But Drew told me he had to talk to me after the screening, you know, probably about my segment and stuff," Amanda stammered self-consciously, stuffing her notes into her too-small pocketbook.

Why did I tell Hero I'm meeting with Drew about work? What difference could it make to Hero why I'm meeting Drew? Amanda scolded herself.

Hero was silent.

Amanda thought for a moment. It couldn't be possible. Hero hadn't just asked her out, had he? Of course not! You and Hero don't get along, remember? Amanda reminded herself.

"But I'll—I mean we'll—see you tomorrow night, right? You'll be at the Beach Bash after the show airs, won't you? And we can celebrate then—all of us," Amanda chattered on.

Hero's face blanched. Amanda's rebuff was like a bucket of cold water thrown in his face. But there was no way he was going to let Amanda know how much she'd hurt him.

"Yeah, sure. See you tomorrow," Hero remarked nonchalantly.

"Well, then, see you tomorrow," Amanda repeated, backing out of the screening room and heading for Drew's office.

Hero noisily gathered up the last of his notes and flipped off the light switch in the screening room. For a moment he stood in the dark, wanting to tear the place apart.

Even though he didn't really want to, Hero couldn't help glancing over at Amanda and Drew, huddled together in Drew's office. Amanda was leaning over Drew, who was sitting at his desk with the swivel chair tilted backward, showing her some notes. Amanda's hair fell over her shoulder, brushing Drew's neck.

Hero winced at the sight. Without another word, he clattered through the station, slamming the door as he left.

Instead of a celebration dinner with Amanda and the others, Hero was going home to a dark, unhappy house where his mother was closeted in her room, either crying or sleeping. His father, holed up in the living room, would be sleeping in front of the television.

It was a familiar scene, and, usually, Hero just went up to his room after grabbing a sandwich from the kitchen. But, tonight, Hero's stomach rebelled at the thought.

Hero threw himself onto his motorcycle and roared off, racing around the corner and three quarters of the way down the block. Then he pulled the bike up short, screeching to a halt.

Hero sat silent and still, head bowed, not knowing what to do. He couldn't drive home, not yet. He wasn't ready to face the gloom. But where else was there to go?

Chapter Eleven

"Let's sit on the couch, Amanda. It'll be easier for us to go over my notes there than to have you standing and leaning over my shoulder," Drew suggested amiably.

Touched by Drew's concern, Amanda gladly removed herself to the couch, perching on the edge expectantly.

Clipboard and notepad in hand, Drew sat down beside Amanda, leaned back against the sagging upholstery, and passed his hand over his eyes.

"Oh, Drew, if you're too tired to go over this stuff tonight, we can just sit and talk for a while—and we can do the work some other time," Amanda offered hopefully.

Drew sat up straight, shaking off his momentary show of fatigue.

"I'm not really tired, Amanda—just a lot of things going on at once," Drew assured her. "But that's got nothing to do with us! So let's get down to it. As I said earlier, I think you all did a really professional job, especially in such a short period of time. And I was very impressed with your fashion satire idea," Drew continued. "It was really brilliant."

Amanda glowed with pride. But niggling at the back of Amanda's mind was the realization that some of the credit for her show went to Hero for his suggestion that she do something funny.

"Now, that aside, there are just a couple of other things we need to talk about . . ." Drew began, shifting closer to Amanda.

Here was the moment Amanda had been living for. Brushing all thoughts of Hero aside, Amanda readied herself for this moment.

Over the past few days, Amanda had wondered when she and Drew were ever going to get around to talking about *them*. Amanda just knew that Drew had been feeling something special for her all along, and she'd been dying for a way to let him know how much she cared. Now Drew was going to take her in his arms and tell her how much he loved her, and how he couldn't bear ever to be apart.

"Yes, Drew?" Amanda asked expectantly, running her tongue lightly over her lips. Her violet eyes glittered in the light.

"The only thing I would keep in mind for next time," Drew said, "is to keep the staging simpler. You and Keera modeling clothes against such a variety of backgrounds

132

detracted from the clothes themselves and the statement you're making."

Amanda started to wilt.

Checking his notes, Drew continued, "And the lighting got a little uneven when you spliced together all those different locations."

"Oh," Amanda said quietly, withdrawing slightly from Drew's side.

"And although women's fashions are what people generally expect, you didn't include anything on men's fashions. Perhaps that's an idea you'll want to pursue for another segment," Drew finished with a flourish.

"Men's clothes, uh—that's a good idea," Amanda answered flatly.

"Well, that about wraps it up," Drew said briskly, flashing Amanda another bright smile as he glanced quickly at his watch.

Amanda was feeling a bit numb. Was that really all Drew had wanted to say?

"By the way, Amanda. You and Hero seem to have worked out your earlier difficulties," Drew said, crossing to his desk and packing up some papers.

Surprised at Drew's statement, Amanda replied hesitantly, "Why, sure, I guess."

Suddenly, a horrible thought occurred to Amanda. Perhaps Drew was holding back from her because he thought she and Hero were together.

133

"But it's a strictly professional relationship," Amanda hastened to assure Drew.

"Well, I'm glad to hear that," Drew said, throwing Amanda an amused glance.

At Drew's remark, the hope in Amanda's heart burned anew.

Drew put the last file into his briefcase and snapped the overstuffed case shut. "Shall we go?" Drew asked her, suddenly animated. With a sweep of his arm, he directed Amanda to the door. "After you, my lady," Drew joked.

Once again feeling cherished and very grown-up, Amanda looked up into Drew's laughing blue eyes and smiled back. Stepping gaily in front of him, Amanda left the station.

As they walked outside into the still summer afternoon, Drew took Amanda's chin between his thumb and forefinger and looked straight into her eyes. He gave her a wonderful, tender smile.

Drew said quietly, "I just want you to know, Amanda . . . that . . ." Drew stopped for a moment.

"Yes?" Amanda asked breathlessly, afraid to move a muscle lest she break the spell.

"Well, I'm very proud of you, Amanda. Don't take my comments too much to heart. You've done a wonderful job—an amazing first effort."

Amanda's face fell. This was it? Great job.

Good work. Good show. What about "I love you," "I need you," and "I can't live without you"?

Not noticing Amanda's crestfallen look, Drew looked at his watch and said, "Gosh, I'm late. I'll see you at the Beach Bash tomorrow, Amanda. I'm hoping to have a wonderful surprise for you then. Perhaps we'll really have something to celebrate!" Drew gently touched her shoulder, then folded his large frame into his Saab and left Amanda standing on the sidewalk as his car sputtered down the street.

Amanda followed Drew's car with her eyes. What was that all about? Amanda wondered, baffled by Drew's abrupt departure.

Walking slowly toward her own car, Amanda contemplated the last few minutes with Drew. He had looked at her so tenderly, she thought. Amanda's skin prickled into goose bumps at the memory of Drew's fingers on her face.

Getting into her car, Amanda pushed the top down and briefly checked her reflection in the mirror. Her face burned against the coldness of her clammy hands. Examining herself critically in the mirror, Amanda thought that she looked the same, not at all like what she pictured herself: a mature woman involved in an important relationship with an older man.

Then Amanda remembered Drew's promise that he had a surprise for her and that they would celebrate at the Beach Bash. Amanda decided that Drew must be waiting for the perfect moment to tell her how he felt. He was right, Amanda thought to herself, starting up her Mustang. The setting for their moment should be perfect, not the cracked sidewalk outside the cable station.

Tomorrow night she'd be dancing in Drew's arms, listening to him murmur against her hair how much he loved her, Amanda thought as she slowly drove off.

Still, she wished there was someone with whom she could talk about Drew. She didn't want to lay this on Keera again. Maybe I'll stop at the Snack Shack and look for Samantha, Amanda thought. She had already told Samantha about Drew, down to the minutest detail—even what color socks he wore each day. Samantha must have some words of wisdom, Amanda thought wryly. After all, she had plenty of experience.

Absorbed in her thoughts, Amanda didn't notice Hero, still sitting motionless on his Harley.

But Hero noticed—first Drew's car, and then Amanda's following after it. With a scowl, Hero gunned his motorcycle and took off in the opposite direction.

Chapter Twelve

After leaving the KSS station, Jamar pedaled around, looking for Keera. She had seemingly disappeared from view before he had even gotten out the door.

Finally, Jamar spotted Keera on a seldom-traveled side street. She didn't know how to feel when she heard Jamar speed up beside her.

"You're a hard woman to track," Jamar said, puffing slightly.

"Uh, I'm kind of in a hurry, Jamar," Keera told him, not wanting to look into Jamar's eyes. Instead, she focused on the cracks in the sidewalk as she kept on walking.

"Listen, Keera, about the other day. I wanted to ask you something, but then things got a little complicated," Jamar began to say.

Keera stiffened, and her eyes filled. "Is that what you call it, complicated?" she asked, trying to control the trembling in her voice.

Stunned, Jamar dropped his bike and ran in front of Keera, blocking her path.

"What's up with you, girl?" Jamar asked, genuinely concerned. "Is something bothering you that I don't know about?"

"Something's bothering me, all right," Keera said in a low voice, still refusing to meet Jamar's eyes.

"Talk to me, Keera," Jamar said, standing firm.

"Talking, that's right. That's what you're good at," Keera said angrily, trying to get past him.

"Keera, girl, please tell me what's bugging you," Jamar pleaded. He reached to take hold of Keera's arms, but she wriggled out of his grasp and took to the street, leaving him, arms empty, on the sidewalk.

"Keera, you're breaking my heart," Jamar called after her.

At that, Keera whirled around, furious. "*I'm* breaking *your* heart? Go find your little girlfriend and ask her to take care of it," Keera said. She was angry with herself for revealing her feelings. I wasn't going to do this, Keera thought, biting her lip.

Jamar stood completely still. "Girlfriend —what? Keera, what are you talking about?" he asked.

"Jamar Williams, do you think I'm a fool?" Keera asked, hands on her hips. She'd never done anything like this before, but she was angrier than she'd ever been in her life.

"I suppose that cute little girl you had your arms around last Friday was a figment of my imagination? An old friend in trouble?"

Jamar looked puzzled for a moment. Then he realized who Keera was talking about, and he tried to explain. But Keera wasn't about to give him the chance.

"Or, I know, maybe she was an imaginary sister, or perhaps your poor old mother? Well, I don't think so. So don't pretend to me that we have anything to say to each other unless we're talking about work, 'cause we don't," Keera finished with a flourish, amazed at the sound of her own voice.

Unexpectedly, Jamar burst out laughing.

Keera had definitely not been expecting him to laugh. Bend his head, act ashamed, get angry, shrug and walk away, yes. But laughing—she didn't know what to think.

"You think this is funny?" Keera asked in disbelief. Furious again, she turned and started to walk off as fast as she could.

Trying to control his laughter, Jamar ran over to her.

"Keera, wait up. No, it's not funny. That girl you saw me with, she *is* my sister," Jamar told her.

"What?" Keera asked, uncertain now.

Jamar put his hands on Keera's shoulders and looked steadily into her face. Keera's skin tingled beneath his touch as an electric current began to hum through her body. Halfheartedly, Keera moved out from under Jamar's hold. Jamar's hands hung suspended in the air beside Keera. Jamar didn't know what to do with them or where to put them.

"Keera, it's true. You saw me with Jolie, my half sister. She's only fourteen, going on twenty-one—as my mother says," Jamar added.

"The other day, when we were talking, you never said anything about a half sister. You said it was just you and your mother," Keera said slowly, wanting to believe Jamar.

"Jolie lives with her dad most of the year. She just lives with us in the summer. And this summer things have already gotten too hot to handle."

Jamar explained about the fight between Jolie and his mother, Jolie's running away, and the phone call at work.

Keera felt like a total fool.

"I'm sorry, Jamar. I don't know why I

140

acted like that. After all, it's not my business what you do or with whom, anyway," Keera apologized.

"Girl, it's definitely your business," Jamar said in a low, husky voice that thrilled Keera. "Everything about me is your business. There's nothing and nobody that matters more to me," Jamar assured her, tenderly removing her glasses and looking deep into her eyes.

"Do you hear me, pretty Keera?" Jamar asked her, gently stroking the wisps of hair that had struggled loose from her ponytail, sending chills down her spine.

Gazing up into Jamar's open face, Keera wanted to believe him. She examined his eyes, so big and dark, desperately searching for some sign of encouragement.

Solemnly, Keera reached up with her hand and lightly touched his cheek. Jamar's hand closed around hers. He brought her hand to his lips, and, still gazing into Keera's sea-green eyes, he kissed it.

The street faded away. Keera saw nothing but Jamar's face, as she tenderly traced his soft lips with her finger. Some invisible force drew their bodies closer and closer together. Keera tilted her head up and closed her eyes, waiting for the electric moment when their lips would meet.

Suddenly, they were interrupted by the roar of a motorcycle, swerving to a halt within inches of where they were standing. Jamar grabbed Keera and pulled her over to the curb out of harm's way.

"What's with you, man?" Jamar said angrily, turning to see who was on the bike.

Pulling off his helmet, Hero jumped from his cycle. He ran over to the curb to make sure Keera and Jamar were all right.

"I'm sorry, Jam," Hero apologized. "I'm sorry, Keera. I was thinking about stuff, and I was mad, as usual. I didn't see you guys in the road until it was almost too late." He ran his hands through his hair, shaking. To calm himself, he sat back on his heels near the curb.

Jamar shook his head. "You gotta look where you're going, man. You could have been the one who got hurt."

"I know, Jam, I know," Hero said, rocking back and forth on his heels, holding onto his elbows as if he could keep himself from flying apart. "It's just that everything's coming down on me all at once," he said shakily. "But that's no excuse for almost killing you guys."

Keera put her hand on Jamar's arm, and they exchanged a secret look of understanding.

"Forget it, dude," Jamar said, slapping Hero on the shoulder in a friendly way. "Hey, Hero, Keera and I were just about to get something to eat—maybe at that Snack Shack where the rich kids go, over near the Bluff," Jamar said quickly, looking over at Keera for confirmation.

"That's right," Keera said. "Why don't you come with us for kind of a pre-celebration dinner?"

Looking from one to the other, Hero shook his head. "Nah, you guys go ahead. I'd just be in the way."

"No, man, you wouldn't be in the way. And we all have to eat, right?" Jamar said.

Hero looked at Keera. She was smiling her encouragement. And Jamar looked like he really meant what he said.

"Sure, I'd love to grab something to eat," Hero said gratefully. "How about a ride, Keera?" he offered. "I promise to watch where I'm going," he added with an impish grin.

Looking over at Jamar, Keera nodded, then tentatively climbed onto the motorcycle behind Hero.

"Take good care, bro—that's *my* lady you've got there," Jamar said, placing Keera's glasses gently back on her nose before turning to pick up his bike.

"Absolutely," Hero said, pulling on his helmet. "See you there."

Holding tightly to Hero's waist, Keera squeezed her eyes shut as the motorcycle roared off in the direction of the Snack Shack. She had never been on a motorcycle before, and she wasn't sure she ever wanted to be on one again. Opening her eyes for a second, Keera was glad to see that they were only a block away from the Snack Shack.

Hero, intent upon keeping his eyes on the road, didn't notice Amanda's white Mustang pulling out of the restaurant parking lot as he rode up. But she noticed him.

Not finding Samantha at the Snack Shack, Amanda had decided to go straight home. At the roar of a familiar engine, she checked her rearview mirror and caught a glimpse of Hero pulling up to the Snack Shack. Some girl was sitting behind Hero, with her arms around his waist.

Well, it didn't take long for him to find someone else to celebrate with, Amanda thought, feeling a slight pang of . . . of . . . she didn't know what. What's wrong with me? Amanda wondered. What's it to me if Hero goes out with someone? It's Drew I should be thinking about, not Hero.

Annoyed with herself, Amanda gunned the engine and drove off toward home.

Chapter Thirteen

*H*ero and Keera walked into the half-empty Snack Shack. It was too early for the regular crowd to be hanging around, so there were plenty of empty booths. Hero and Keera picked a purple table with blue vinyl seats, close enough to the door so they could watch for Jamar.

Keera ordered a salad and a diet soda.

Hero eyed the prices on the menu. They were two or three dollars higher than any other burger joint in town. But, hey, this was a celebration, wasn't it? So Hero splurged and ordered a double-chili cheeseburger, atomic fries, and a triple-thick chocolate shake.

Keera shook her head at the order, remembering that that was exactly what Amanda had eaten.

"What's wrong?" Hero asked, laughing. "I'm a growing boy."

"Nothing. It's just that's exactly what Amanda ordered when we came here the other day," Keera said.

145

At the mention of Amanda's name, Hero's face darkened.

Just then, Jamar burst into the Snack Shack, larger than life in his biking gloves, headset, and baseball cap. He was in a happy mood, and he wanted everyone to know it.

"Hey, dude, hey, lovely lady. It was hard keeping up with the two of you," Jamar said, sliding into the seat next to Keera.

Keera smiled happily. It felt good being with Jamar now that she knew he wasn't involved with someone else. Keera felt as if a big, dark cloud had been lifted from her mind.

Catching Keera's smile, Jamar looked right into her eyes and smiled back. For a second, they were the only two people in the world—until the waitress came over and asked Jamar whether he was ready to order.

"I'll have what she's having," Jamar said automatically, still looking at Keera.

"You want a salad and diet soda, that right?" the waitress asked.

Jamar wrinkled his nose. "Uh—on second thought, that sounds way too healthy for me. I'll just have a . . . burger with chili fries and a regular Coke."

Hero laughed out loud, glad that he'd

come along with Jamar and Keera. It definitely beat a dried-out ham sandwich at home, and the atmosphere at the Snack Shack was a lot cheerier. He was almost beginning to feel like he belonged somewhere.

Relaxing against the stiffly upholstered back of the booth, Hero listened as Jamar and Keera chattered about the show and what their families and friends would say when they saw it. While they spoke, the Snack Shack door swung open and shut many times, and a constant stream of Cliffside High kids trickled in until the Shack was buzzing.

Then the door swung open wide, slamming against the wall, so that everyone turned to see who was entering. It was Tyler Scott and Samantha Walker. Tyler, dressed in pressed khakis and an ice-blue polo to match his eyes, with a white tennis sweater thrown casually over his shoulder, stepped into the room like he owned the ground he walked on. Samantha followed a little self-consciously behind him.

As Tyler and Samantha strutted through the Snack Shack, kids at the other tables waved and called "Hi" to them. Tyler nodded shortly, like royalty accepting adulation from the peasants, Hero thought bitterly. Samantha just giggled and smiled, following closely at Tyler's elbow.

Tyler looked back and forth over the Shack, checking out who was there, where they were sitting, and who was sitting with whom. He headed for his usual booth, not expecting anyone to be in it. But when he got there, Tyler's eyes locked onto Hero's. For a moment, neither said or did a thing.

Never one to waste a flirtatious opportunity, especially if it might make Tyler jealous, Samantha batted her lashes at Hero and said in a soft voice, "Oh, hi, Hero. I never expected to run into you here."

"Life's like that," Hero commented lightly, not taking his eyes from Tyler.

"Hey man, how's it going?" Jamar asked Tyler, hoping to douse the fire that was smoking in Tyler's and Hero's eyes.

Tyler ignored him.

Samantha was tired of this macho standoff. She just wanted to sit down. Everyone in the Shack was watching them now, and Samantha wanted them to see Tyler paying attention to her, not Hero.

"Tyler, I'm going to faint from hunger if we don't sit down," Samantha told him.

"But, of course," Tyler said charmingly, reluctantly breaking off his gaze from Hero's and turning to Samantha. "Your appetite is legendary," Tyler added, making Samantha blush.

Then, playing to the crowd, Tyler bowed elaborately.

"Forgive me, Samantha. I was so dazzled by the sight of the local TV celebrities who've deigned to grace our humble establishment that I forgot my manners," Tyler said loudly, his voice oozing with sarcasm.

Hero didn't move a muscle. He didn't even blink. It was taking all the control he had to keep from standing up to Tyler and smashing his face into tomorrow.

"Thanks, man. Good to know you're a fan," Jamar said jokingly, hoping to break the tension.

"See you at the Beach Bash, hotshot," Tyler challenged Hero, ignoring Jamar completely.

Hero tensed, about to rise from his seat and go after Tyler. Then Jamar's surprisingly steely fingers locked onto Hero's arm.

Hero turned a menacing gaze at Jamar's hand.

Jamar lifted his hand up in surrender. "All gone," he quipped, smiling at Hero.

Smirking, Tyler led Samantha over to a table on the other side of the Shack. Once again, voices began to hum.

"Don't do that to me again, Jam," Hero

said quietly. "Next time, I won't lie down and take it."

Keera let out a shaky breath. Amanda had told her that Tyler and Hero couldn't stand each other, but watching them together was something else. No wonder Amanda had been upset.

Pushing away his half-eaten burger, Hero said quietly, "I'm done, you guys. And I'm outta here." He fished in his pocket for some money to cover his tab.

"Hey, be cool, bro. You can't let a guy like Tyler make you get up and go until you're ready and done. His daddy might own a lot of this town, but that doesn't mean a thing. So finish your food, and don't let him know he's getting to you. Because once he knows that, he'll own you, too," Jamar said, eyes level with Hero's.

Keera stole an admiring look at Jamar. There were depths to this guy she'd yet to discover.

"Besides, you've got the power of television behind you. You'll get the best of that dude yet," Jamar reminded Hero with a twinkle in his eyes.

Hero cocked his head at Jamar. He had to admit he respected this guy. Jamar had a way of turning something heavy into no big deal. It was a talent Hero lacked.

Relaxing his tensed muscles, Hero picked up his triple-thick shake and held it up to Jamar and Keera.

"To tomorrow's show," Hero said solemnly.

"Amen to that," Jamar said, holding up his Coke.

"And again," Keera echoed, holding up her diet drink.

Hero downed the rest of his shake in one gulp. But he couldn't help one last sidelong look over at Tyler. Just glimpsing his nasty face made Hero's blood boil.

"Hero, we're over here," Keera said insistently.

With an effort, Hero turned his attention back to his friends.

"I know. It's just I can't help hating guys like that. There's always a guy like that, a crowd like this, and girls like Samantha . . . and Amanda," Hero added bitterly.

"Come on, Hero, that's not fair. Amanda's not like them," Keera protested, remembering her sleepover at Amanda's last week and the way they'd giggled and talked for hours into the night.

"Yeah, I think you've got the chick all wrong," Jamar added. "First of all, Amanda wouldn't be working at a rinky-dink cable station like KSS if she didn't want to. She sure doesn't need the money."

"Can you see Tyler doing that?" Keera chimed in.

Deep in his heart, Hero knew Amanda wasn't like Tyler or his crowd. But Hero also knew that Amanda would never be his, and that hurt so bad, he wanted to hate her, just like he hated those other kids.

"Maybe Amanda isn't like them," Hero admitted slowly. "To tell you the truth, I know she isn't. It's just . . . aw, forget it." Talking about his feelings wasn't something Hero did very often. And the pity in Keera and Jamar's eyes was too much for him to bear.

Sliding out of the booth, Hero left his money on the table.

"See you, folks," he said, shrugging on his leather motorcycle jacket.

"Wait up, we'll be out of here pronto, too," Jamar said. He pulled crumpled bills from here and there, while Keera methodically counted out her money.

Hero sauntered slowly across the length of the Shack, smoothly navigating the tables and chairs as if he'd done it a hundred times. He was aware that everyone's eyes followed him as he went.

Hero stopped for a moment at Tyler's table, and his eyes smouldered. Tyler returned Hero's stare with one of his own.

"See you tomorrow at the Bash, Hero?" Samantha asked flirtatiously, hoping for a jealous spark from Tyler.

"Tomorrow," Hero said quietly, as if to answer Samantha. But his gaze never wavered from Tyler's.

"I'm looking forward to it," Tyler said.

Jamar and Keera caught up to Hero then, and Hero stepped toward the door. There was no reason for Jamar and Keera to know that he and Tyler had just made plans of their own for tomorrow's party.

Outside the Shack, Hero pulled on his helmet and straddled his motorcycle. Seeing Jamar and Keera standing together like they were in their own private world made him wince.

Hero gunned the engine. "Later," he called over his shoulder and rocketed out of the parking lot.

Jamar unlocked his bike. Then he turned to Keera and slipped an arm around her shoulders. Jamar was happier than he could ever remember being. Leaning her head against Jamar's arm, Keera felt just the same.

Thinking of tomorrow, Tyler, and Amanda, Hero had never felt worse.

Chapter Fourteen

July Fourth started out foggy and dreary. Peering anxiously at the overcast afternoon sky, Amanda walked slowly down the tiled steps to her pool, her towel dangling over her shoulder. Amanda had finally been able to sleep late and have a lazy day lounging around the house for what seemed like the first time in months. School was done, the show was a wrap, and she felt like summer hadn't yet begun.

Amanda was hoping to get some sun before tonight's Beach Bash. After two solid weeks of working on the show, Amanda thought she was looking a little pasty.

Amanda stretched her long, sleek legs out on the elegant cast-iron lounge chair. She gazed distractedly at the cloudy afternoon mist that hung above the shoreline several miles away. The sun had been struggling to burn through the fog all day.

Optimistically, Amanda leaned back against the dark green canvas pillow, her long hair fanning out around her head like a wreath. She closed her eyes, listening to the sounds of water cascading down the rock waterfall at the far end of the pool.

Once again, yesterday's conversation with Drew at the studio came to mind. Tonight was the night, she decided. Tonight Drew was going to make his move.

Letting her mind drift into a half-sleep, Amanda daydreamed about what it would be like to be with Drew. She imagined herself all dressed up, sparkling with sequins and jewels, going to expensive restaurants, cool parties, celebrated events—maybe even the Emmys, or the Grammys. Drew had mentioned that he had a close friend who worked at Rock America on HIP-TV with whom he went to both events every year.

Amanda imagined that she and Drew were about to introduce this year's winners of a new-category Emmy: Best Amateur Programming. Coincidentally, the winners turned out to be none other than Amanda, Keera, Jamar, and . . . Hero.

Biting her lip, Amanda tried to expel Hero from her mind. But the harder she tried, the more his face loomed before her. She saw images of Hero shaking out his hair when he took off his helmet, Hero standing against the brilliant blue sky on the football field at Cliffside High, his hair blowing slightly in the breeze, standing defiantly against Tyler and the team. She flushed again at the memory of how angry he had been with her. But then, as if nothing had ever happened, there was Hero smiling at her after watching the screening of their show, asking her if she wanted to celebrate together.

Unbidden, the unpleasant memory of Hero riding up in the Snack Shack parking lot with some girl's arms around his waist popped into Amanda's mind. That still bothered her, and she couldn't figure out why. After all, why should it matter to her if Hero had someone else with whom he wanted to celebrate?

Shivering again, even though the sun had come out, Amanda decided to think only happy thoughts—about the show, which would air in a few hours, about what she was going to wear to the Bash, and, of course, about Drew and how he would fold her into his arms and hold her there forever when they met at the Bash.

"Amanda!" Mrs. Townsend called from the patio.

Amanda woke with a start from her sun-hazed reverie.

"Amanda, it's 5:00. You've been out in the sun for almost an hour—I hope you had sunscreen on," Mrs. Townsend said sharply. "Shouldn't you be thinking about getting

157

dressed for the party at the Club this evening? I picked up a dress and left it on your bed. Amanda, did you hear me?"

That was a silly question—Amanda could hear her mother's voice anywhere. Checking her watch to see that it was, indeed, 5:00 already, Amanda picked up her towel and started for the house.

The show was airing at 6:00 that evening, and the Beach Bash started at 7:30. Amanda would have just enough time to get herself ready before seeing the show and getting to the party.

Amanda bounded up the wide, carpeted stairs two at a time. She stopped halfway down the hall, remembering that her mother thought she was joining her at the Club party this evening, and headed back toward her mother's room.

"Mom, I'm not going with you to the Club, remember? This year I'm going to the Beach Bash with everyone to celebrate my show," Amanda told her.

"Oh, that's right, you did mention that," Mrs. Townsend replied as she walked around her room, assembling her outfit for the evening.

"Are you and Dad going to catch my show?" Amanda asked. "It's on at 6:00, and my fashion spoof is up first."

Mrs. Townsend never took her eyes from

158

the mirror as she spoke to Amanda's reflection in the glass. "A fashion spoof? What is that exactly?" she asked.

"You know, showing how we've all become slaves to fashion designers, no matter how ridiculous the outfit, and how we've lost our sense of individuality," Amanda said pointedly, looking at the two designer dresses her mother was choosing between.

"Oh," Mrs. Townsend said, refusing to take Amanda's bait. "Well, your father and I can watch the show for a few minutes. But you know they serve cocktails promptly at 6:00 at the Club."

Amanda's eyes slid away from her mother's reflection.

"What's happening at 6:00?" Amanda's father asked, coming up behind Amanda and giving her a careless kiss on the top of her head.

"Dad, hi!" Amanda brightened. Her father wasn't home much, but she loved it when he was. "Remember I told you about my summer job, working for KSS? Well, the show's on tonight, at 6:00."

"Then of course we'll watch it before we go," Mr. Townsend said decisively.

"Thanks, Daddy," Amanda said, pecking him on the cheek as she made a mad dash to her room to dress for the party.

At two minutes to six, Amanda rushed into the downstairs television room, calling to her mother and father to join her. She switched on the television and perched herself on the arm of the black leather couch, trying not to wrinkle the delicate, creamy lace of the long dress her mother had bought her. She loved it even though her mother had chosen it.

As the opening credits with Jamar's music came on, Amanda's father and mother came into the room.

"Amanda, I bought you that dress to wear to the Club, not to a beach party," Mrs. Townsend complained.

"Oh, Mom, it's so pretty, I just had to wear it tonight," Amanda told her. Then Mr. Townsend hushed them both as Amanda's image flashed on the screen.

Watching herself, Amanda squirmed. It was different somehow, seeing herself in the screening room at the studio and watching herself on television at home.

Mrs. Townsend watched the program distractedly, checking her watch every few minutes and rearranging its gold-link chain on her wrist. Mr. Townsend laughed at all the right times. As her segment came to a close, he came over and gave Amanda a quick hug.

"Did you really like it, Dad?" Amanda wanted to know.

"You were great, honey," Mr. Townsend told her sincerely.

Then he glanced over at Mrs. Townsend, who was waiting impatiently at the door.

"What did you think, Mom?" Amanda asked.

"It was very good, dear. Although I would have thought you'd have done something a little bit more interesting than just putting on different outfits."

Amanda sighed in frustration. She couldn't please her mother, not in this life.

Mr. Townsend gave Amanda a sympathetic look. "Have a good time tonight, Amanda," he called over his shoulder.

"Don't ruin your dress at the beach," Mrs. Townsend added as she got into the car.

Then the phone started ringing. For the next forty-five minutes, try as she might to watch the other segments, Amanda was unable to get off the phone as everyone she knew called to say they'd loved her show. Even Samantha called to tell Amanda the segment had been fabulous.

Amanda glowed with pride. Then call-waiting clicked and Amanda told Samantha she had to go. She thought that Drew might be on the other end of the line. But when she picked up, there was no one there at all.

Amanda replaced the sleek black phone in

its cradle. With a sigh, she decided to give up hope of hearing from Drew until she got to the Beach Bash. All the wishful thinking in the world wasn't going to make Drew's call happen.

Checking her reflection in the hall mirror, Amanda straightened her brown velvet choker with the drop pearl. She smoothed down her dress, feeling the satiny inner lining settle against her skin.

Bending her head forward, Amanda gave her shining hair one last flurry of brushes, then threw her head back so that her hair billowed around her.

Satisfied that Drew would be totally happy with the way she looked, Amanda headed for her Mustang. Tonight was going to be a wonderful night. Amanda just knew it.

Keera's day had started early and showed no sign of ending. She'd spent the whole day babysitting her two younger cousins while their mother, who worked at the local department store, helped out with the big Fourth of July sale.

Swinging the two little girls at the neighborhood park, Keera sighed dreamily. She was remembering last night's walk home with Jamar, their fingers intertwined, their arms touching.

They had stopped under a street lamp a few blocks from Keera's house. Jamar had looked straight into Keera's sea-green eyes, his own eyes shining in the dark.

Slowly, Jamar bent his head down, and Keera closed her eyes, holding her breath. Jamar gently touched his lips to hers. Then he brought Keera close to him, folding her body into his. She could feel his hard, lean chest against her own softly yielding frame.

"Oh, Keera," Jamar had whispered into her hair.

"Keera, Keera, we want to get down, we want to get down."

The squealing voices of the two little girls broke into her thoughts. Keera had been swinging them higher and higher, unaware that they had been telling her they wanted to get down for the last five minutes.

"Okay, okay," Keera said patiently, slowing the swings down and helping them off.

Let loose from the swings, the two little girls catapulted toward the slide. Keera followed them, trying to pay attention to their chatter.

But the playground kept fading away to last night.

When Keera and Jamar had finally reached Keera's front door, they'd stood looking deeply into each other's eyes for what seemed like forever. All the world stood still as Jamar encircled Keera with one arm, drawing her nearer and nearer. Keera never wanted him to leave, never wanted this moment to end.

Then she closed her eyes, offering up her mouth.

Jamar's face was within inches of hers, his other hand lightly caressing her cheek, her hair. Keera felt herself melting inside as Jamar pulled her tightly against him. She tasted Jamar's lips on hers.

Then the porch light flickered on, the front door was yanked open, and Keera's seven-year-old brother, Akim, stood accusingly in the doorway.

"Hey, girl, where have you been?" Akim began. Then he noticed Jamar, and his mouth dropped open.

"You little . . . " Keera said, stepping toward Akim, angry and mortified at the same time.

Akim, having scoped out the situation, stuck out his tongue and jeered, "Keera's got a boyfriend, Keera's got a boyfriend." Then he hightailed it up the narrow wooden stairs to his room, tripping over sneakers, clothes, and toys that he'd left on the staircase, but never actually falling on his face.

"Cute kid," Jamar said, crinkling his eyes in the way that Keera loved.

"Yeah, sometimes. Not at the moment."

"Well, I better be going, anyway," Jamar had said then, touching her face lightly with his fingers before backing down the porch steps. "See you tomorrow at the Bash, girlfriend."

"See you tomorrow," Keera had echoed, smiling as she watched Jamar moonwalk backward to make her laugh.

Keera smiled again at the memory. Her cousins, seeing that Keera wasn't paying any attention to them, dumped cups of ice-cold water that they'd scooped up from the park fountain onto her sandaled feet. The water sure got her attention. Keera yelped, and the two little girls giggled.

Then, hearing the church bells ring five times, Keera realized how late it was. She'd spent practically the whole afternoon at the park and she hadn't even noticed. It was time to get the girls back for her aunt to collect them, and just enough time to get ready before the show aired.

"Okay, you two, back to my house," Keera said amidst their protests, shepherding them down the street.

"Honey, where have you been with those girls all afternoon?" Keera's mother asked, hands on hips. "You better hurry and get cleaned up. It's almost time for your show and that Beach Bash of yours."

Keera ran up to shower and change before the show came on. By 5:45, she was back downstairs, dressed in a pretty 1940s dress that had once belonged to her grandmother. The dress flowed around Keera's ankles, the tiny bright peach flowers against their soft white background highlighting the warm coral of her painted toenails, which peeked out through her white leather sandals.

"My, my, Keera, girl, don't you look pretty!" Aunt Ruth exclaimed.

Keera could tell from his shining eyes that even Akim thought Keera looked nice. But she knew he wouldn't admit it, not even under tickle torture.

Then Keera's whole family gathered around the television. Akim and his two little cousins squirmed against each other, vying for the best seat in the house. Keera's older brother, Malcolm, and his girlfriend Tracy were there, along with Aunt Ruth and a couple of the neighbors. Mr. and Mrs. Johnson smiled proudly as they all waited expectantly for Keera's show to come on.

It was two minutes before six when the doorbell rang. Everyone looked at Keera.

"Are you expecting anyone, honey?" Mrs. Johnson finally asked.

Keera hurried to the door to see who was there. She hadn't been expecting anyone, but maybe . . .

Jamar was standing at the door, looking all polished in his new green army pants and a crisp white shirt.

Keera opened the door wide, smiling happily.

"Hey, Keera, you look like something, girl." Jamar whistled in admiration.

"What are you doing here?" Keera asked, surprised and pleased at the same time. "I thought we were going to meet at the Beach Bash."

"Thought I'd rather watch our show with you than with my mother and Jolie. They're always fighting, and I probably wouldn't be able to hear anything if I watched it with them, anyway," Jamar said, stepping into the house.

"Who is it, honey?" Mrs. Johnson called.

"Uh, a friend of mine from work, Ma. Jamar Williams," Keera replied, trying to sound nonchalant.

Akim spotted Jamar and started to giggle. He nudged his two little cousins, who screamed delightedly, "Keera's got a boyfriend, Keera's got a boyfriend!"

Giving Akim a look that could kill, Keera blushed right down to the roots of her soft brown hair.

Jamar jumped right in.

"She does?" he asked, looking around in

surprise. "Where is he? Let me at him," he teased, smiling at the little girls.

"Well, come over here, quick. Your show's about to start," Mrs. Johnson called, eyeing Jamar as he entered the living room and took his place in front of the television. With one eye on the show and the other on Jamar, Mrs. Johnson proudly watched Keera's name roll across the screen.

Everyone sat spellbound, watching Keera's spot. When it was over, Mr. and Mrs. Johnson beamed.

Jamar's eyes shone at Keera, and she knew how happy he was for her. She smiled back at him, glad that he'd come over to watch the show with her family.

"Keera, girl, that was a fine piece of work," Mr. Johnson said solemnly.

"Something to be proud of," Mrs. Johnson said, wiping a tear from the corner of her eye.

"Oh, Ma," Keera said with an exasperated tone. She hated when her mother got all weepy over nothing.

When Jamar's "Jammin'" came on, one of the little cousins screamed, "Hey, you're on television, too," pointing at Jamar.

"That stuff is smokin'," Malcolm said to Jamar in admiration.

When Hero's "Flip Side" segment came on, Mr. Johnson and his two sons burst out laughing. "Cliffside's certainly had some serious problems with their football," Malcolm said. Malcolm went to Stanford University, so he hadn't followed high school sports in some time.

As the show drew to a close and Keera's name rolled over the screen again, her mother and father came over and hugged her. They were so proud Keera thought they might burst.

Jamar was talking music with Malcolm when Keera came over and nudged him. "Don't you think it's time to go?" Keera asked. She didn't want to get roped into eating dinner with the family. And from the way Jamar was acting, she was afraid she would never get him out of her house.

Just then the telephone rang. It was for Jamar.

"For me?" Jamar asked with surprise.

Keera watched Jamar's face anxiously as he went to the telephone. Her heart ached as she remembered the last time Jamar had gotten an unexpected phone call. She wondered if they'd ever make it to the Beach Bash at all.

Keera strained to hear Jamar's half of the conversation. "What's up? Say what? Yeah, it was. Sure. Cool. Definitely. Very cool, man. Later."

Then Jamar hung up. "Ready to go, Keera?" he asked.

"What was that phone call about?" Keera

asked Jamar as they were driving to the Beach Bash in his mother's car.

"Oh, it was Rogue."

"Rogue?" Keera asked, her stomach sinking. "Is something wrong?" Keera wondered if Rogue was planning some way to keep Jamar and her apart. He hadn't made his dislike of her much of a secret, at least not to Keera.

"Not a thing. I had told him I'd be watching our show at your house and gave him your number. Was that okay?"

"Sure," Keera said faintly, not wanting Jamar to know how much she distrusted Rogue. "So, what did he have to say?"

"Oh, he just wanted to let me know about a little surprise we've got cooking, that's all," Jamar said, humming happily to himself.

Keera settled back against the worn fabric of Jamar's mother's car with a shrug. Keera wasn't going to let Rogue Jelsen or anyone else interfere with her happiness tonight.

Hero's Fourth of July hadn't started out too well. His parents had chosen that day to have their biggest argument to date.

"I just want to try working for a while," Mrs. Montoya had said insistently. "What are you so afraid of, Joseph?"

"Afraid? I'm not afraid of anything!" Mr.

Montoya had shouted as he stormed out of the house. Only this time he wasn't going to work. Neither Hero nor his mother knew where he was off to.

Hero wished his mother hadn't picked today to battle it out over getting a job. And he wished that his father could see that his mother needed to get out of the house. Hero felt sorry for them both, but he was angry at them, too. This was a really big day for him, and neither one of them seemed to care about anything but themselves.

Hero patted his mother's shoulder awkwardly as the tears coursed soundlessly down Mrs. Montoya's cheeks. He felt awful watching his mother cry, knowing there was nothing he could do or say that would make it all right.

After a few minutes, Mrs. Montoya told Hero she was going to lie down for awhile. Then, looking neither to the left or the right, she went into her small, bare bedroom off the kitchen and closed the door.

Hero paced around the kitchen for a few moments, wanting to strike out at something, but not knowing what. He glanced at the hand-painted ceramic kitchen clock, which his mother had gotten as a wedding present and which had hung in every house they'd ever lived in. Two o'clock. His parents had probably forgotten all about Hero's show.

Well, he wasn't going to spend the next few hours banging aimlessly around the house. Hero got out his treasured toolbox, the one his father had given him when he was thirteen years old. He'd rebuilt and amplified the Harley's engine with this toolbox plenty of times before.

Carrying the toolbox out to the garage, Hero automatically started to take apart the Harley's engine and meticulously clean all its parts. It's what he always did when he didn't know what to do with himself and there wasn't anyplace to go. Hero knew it would take him about three hours. That would take care of this afternoon. Then he'd watch the show and drag his act to the Beach Bash.

Maybe he'd even get a chance to start over with Amanda, Hero thought as he got caught up in the mechanical acts of untwisting bolts, unscrewing screws, and oiling and cleaning the one thing in his life that had never let him down.

At 6:00 sharp, Hero was in his living room, sprawled out on the lumpy, floral-covered couch, remote in hand and the television on. He had taken apart and put together the Harley's engine, and he was satisfied that it looked and ran better than new. He'd showered and taken special care blow-drying his hair, letting it fall in soft brown waves above his forehead. His strong arms were crossed behind his head, and his jet-black T-shirt fit tightly over his muscled chest.

Mrs. Montoya entered the living room. "You look like one of those models for jeans," Mrs. Montoya told him, coming over to ruffle his hair.

"Come on, Ma, quit it," Hero said, pulling his head away slightly and keeping his eyes glued to the set. He was glad his mother had come out of her room and was acting normal, but he didn't want to make a big deal about it.

"What are you watching, Hero?" Mrs. Montoya asked.

"You know, Ma, it's the show I've been working on this summer," Hero replied.

"Oh, no. I forgot it was on tonight, what with your father . . . Have I already missed it?" she asked in alarm.

"No, it's just starting." Hero swung his legs off the couch so his mother could sit down.

Together they watched the show in silence. His mother smiled wanly at the funny parts in Amanda's spoof. Hero watched Amanda intently, wishing that somehow they could be together, watching the show with her sitting in the circle of his arms.

Mrs. Montoya grew solemn while watching Keera's portion of the show, but when Jamar's jam session came on, she relaxed a bit. Hero danced around for a few minutes, trying to convince his mother to join him. But she just shook her head, saying she couldn't figure out how to dance to the music kids listened to today.

They both laughed out loud during the "Flip Side," particularly when Tyler slipped and fell in the mud, flinging the football behind him for the other team to score a touchdown. It was good to hear her laugh. It had been a long time.

When the show was over, Hero switched off the television and jumped up. He was torn between feeling like he should stay with his mother and really wanting to go to the beach party.

"Are you going to be all right, Ma?" Hero asked with concern. "I was thinking about going out for a while."

Mrs. Montoya stood up, putting her cool, dry hand on her son's shoulder. "I'll be fine. And I just wanted to tell you that you did a wonderful job with this show. I'm proud of you," she said.

Just then the phone rang sharply, making them both jump.

Hero and his mother stared at the phone, wondering who it could be. Hero picked it up, hoping it was Amanda, even though he knew that was impossible.

His father's voice crackled over the wire, with a television blaring and lots of voices in the background.

"Hero, Hero, can you hear me?" Mr. Montoya asked.

"Yeah, yeah, Dad, I hear you," Hero said hoarsely.

"Son, I saw your show. I remembered it was on, but it was too late to turn around and come home, so I watched it at a bar in town," Mr. Montoya shouted into the phone.

Hero felt the tight knot that had been squeezing his stomach all day loosen a notch. His dad hadn't forgotten about his show after all.

"Your sports piece was great, Hero. The whole show was great." Then, off to the side, Mr. Montoya shouted, "Hey, I'm talking to my son the television reporter. I'll be off in a minute.

"Did you hear me, Hero? You did good," Mr. Montoya shouted again over the bad connection.

"Thanks, Dad. Thanks for watching," Hero said. "Do you want to talk to Mom?" he added, not sure how to handle this whole thing.

"Uh, not right now, Hero. I've gotta go. But I'll be home later, and we'll all sit down and have a talk. All of us, you, me, and your mom. Okay?" Mr. Montoya asked insistently.

"Yeah, that would be okay, Dad," Hero said.

Hero replaced the receiver back on the wall. As he stared at the phone, Amanda's face popped into Hero's mind. Should he call her? Taking a deep breath, he dialed the number, which he had memorized the first day he'd met her.

Then Hero heard his mother crying quietly in her bedroom. He quickly hung up the phone and walked over to her closed door.

"Are you sure you're going to be okay, Ma?" Hero asked.

"Yes, Hero, I'm fine," his mother's muffled voice called from the bedroom. After a few moments, she called in the old motherly voice he was used to, "Don't be too late getting home, son."

Hero knew then that it was okay to go. She was going to be all right—in a while.

Pulling on his helmet and leather jacket, Hero revved the motorcycle engine. His mother looked out the window briefly and waved to him with a tired smile.

She really is beautiful, Hero thought to himself. How could his dad fight with her? Why couldn't he understand her?

Unbidden, Amanda's face floated in front of Hero's eyes again. If she were *mine*, I'd never fight with her, Hero thought grimly to himself.

Somehow he had to make things right between him and Amanda once and for all.

Chapter Fifteen

$\mathcal{B}$y the time Hero roared up to the parking lot, Cliffside's Fourth of July Beach Bash was in full swing.

Checking out the crowded parking lot, Hero saw Amanda's white Mustang and his hopes deflated just a bit. Hero had been hoping to catch Amanda alone before she was surrounded by her usual impenetrable crowd of friends.

Cruising for a spot, Hero noticed a brand new Fatboy Softail Harley parked at the far end of the lot. Hero couldn't resist driving by it. It was beautiful—polished chrome, buttery leather saddle, almost a modern copy of the classic '66 Harley he had rebuilt.

Locking up his own bike and hanging up his helmet, Hero wondered who else at Cliffside was into cycles. He'd never noticed this bike around before.

Walking down the long stretch of sand that separated him from the party, Hero saw that just about everybody from Cliffside

High was already there, knotted in groups, drinks and snacks in hand. Everyone looked like they were having a great time.

Pushing aside a bunch of red, white, and blue balloons and Fourth of July streamers festooning the food stands, Hero grabbed an ice-cold drink from the huge copper cooler piled high with ice and soda cans.

Amanda had been nervously scanning the crowd for Drew from the middle of a group of admirers when she noticed Hero over by the drinks. Holding her breath, Amanda checked to see if Hero had brought anyone with him. It didn't look like he had. She wasn't quite sure why, but she was relieved to see that he'd come by himself.

Just then Keera and Jamar arrived. They spotted Hero right away and made their way through the throng to him.

"Hey, dude, congratulations! Nice show." Jamar stepped up to Hero, slapping him five.

Keera impulsively hugged Hero. Something about the way he'd been standing all alone made her feel protective.

"And to the two of you," Hero said, hugging Keera back and grinning widely at Jamar.

"Have you seen Amanda?" Keera asked, trying to peer over the heads of the people around her.

"No. It's impossible to find anybody around here," Hero said.

"Hey, my man," Rogue came up behind Jamar, slapping him on the back. "Cool show, like I told you on the phone."

"What's up?" Jamar asked Rogue. "Are we on for later?"

"We are, indeed," Rogue replied, giving Keera a contemptuous glance.

Before Keera could ask Jamar what was up, some kids came over and started chattering about how much they loved her segment and asking what they could do to help. Keera answered their questions and thanked them for their support. By the time she turned back to where Jamar and Rogue had been standing, both of them were gone.

Keera was slightly annoyed. She knew that Rogue didn't like her and that he didn't approve of Jamar and her together. But Keera wasn't about to let what Rogue thought get in their way. So where was Jamar? Keera wondered, weaving in and out of the crowd.

Hero had wandered off while Keera talked to her friends. From here and there, kids called "Hey, that's Hero Montoya," or "Hero, funny show." Hero smiled slightly and waved whenever anyone called to him.

He thought it was interesting that suddenly everyone knew his name.

I'm an overnight celebrity, he thought to himself with a small grin.

Just then Hero spotted Amanda in the center of a crowd of girls who were oohing and aahing about her dress.

Amanda looked like an angel, Hero thought to himself. The air around her seemed to dance and her hair gave off a soft, glowing sheen. Her violet eyes shone against her smoothly tanned skin. Hero couldn't remember ever seeing her look as perfect as she did tonight.

Hero realized that he didn't want to spend another minute of his life without her. He had to tell her how he felt, and he had to do it right now.

From the corner of her eye, Amanda caught a glimpse of Hero in his leather jacket and black shirt, his hair blowing in the cool breeze. Amanda's heart stopped for a moment. He really was drop-dead handsome. For some reason, Amanda flushed slightly.

While Hero made his way toward Amanda, a hand clamped down on his arm, preventing him from getting through the crowd. Hero knew before their eyes connected that it would be Tyler Scott.

Hero yanked his arm from Tyler's grasp.

"Don't touch me, man," he said in a cold, low voice between clenched teeth.

"What are you going to do about it?" Tyler asked, chin out, challenging Hero.

Hero caught a glimpse of Amanda in the background, laughing and looking like she was having the time of her life. He knew he wasn't going to fight Tyler, at least not right now.

"Get a life, Tyler," Hero said contemptuously and pushed past him.

"Don't forget. We have a date for later, wiseguy," Tyler replied.

Dismissing Tyler from his mind, Hero moved steadily toward Amanda. Talking to her and trying to get her to understand how he felt about her suddenly seemed like the most important thing he was ever going to do with his life. Nothing and no one else mattered.

As Keera searched the crowd for Jamar, she saw Drew arrive and survey the crowd. He was obviously in a great mood: smiling, confident, looking like he was at home anywhere he went in the world.

He was such a happy-go-lucky kind of guy, Keera thought to herself, smiling and waving at him. He's pretty good-looking, too, even if he is kind of old. I guess I can see why Amanda's so crazy about him.

Then, as Keera watched, Drew turned around and brought forward a . . . a girl . . . no . . . a woman . . . a very attractive woman! Keera couldn't believe her eyes.

Keera looked at this "other woman" critically. She was about Drew's age, maybe a bit older, with short, wavy red hair and luminous green eyes. And she was dressed to kill in a red halter sheath dress. Keera had to admit she looked incredibly sexy.

Keera's mouth dropped open when she saw Drew put his arm around this woman's shoulders, then bring her in close for a kiss, before they started to move, hand in hand, through the crowd.

Amanda is going to lie down and die, Keera thought to herself in a panic. Should she try to find Amanda and warn her? Should she try to keep Amanda from seeing Drew? And where was Jamar? Why wasn't he ever around when she needed him? Keera was annoyed that Jamar would just desert her after making such a big deal about watching the show with her at her house.

Keera pushed her way through the crowd, nodding absently to people who congratulated her on the show. She had to find Amanda before Amanda found Drew.

At long last, Amanda spotted Drew's head above the crowd. Forgetting instantly about Hero's approach, Amanda started to move toward Drew, waving at him to get his attention over the throng of heads that separated them.

Drew caught sight of Amanda and waved back. At that same moment, Amanda caught sight of the woman beside him. The adoring smile that was meant for Drew died on her lips, and the color drained from her face.

I'm sure there's a reasonable explanation, Amanda told herself. Maybe that's his sister. She recalled how Keera had told her about Jamar's half sister Jolie. Smiling brightly, she forced herself to go over to Drew and the redhaired woman.

"Amanda, you look great," Drew said, giving her a friendly hug. Without giving Amanda a chance to reply, Drew turned to his redheaded friend and said, "Zoe, I'd like you to meet Amanda Townsend, one of the most promising young fashion commentators in television!"

Zoe gave Amanda a lovely smile. "It's wonderful to finally meet you, Amanda," Zoe said. "Drew has said so many nice things about all of you working at KSS for the summer." She turned to Drew and added, "You're right, Drew, Amanda does remind me of your kid sister."

"I know, the resemblance is amazing," Drew agreed, turning to Amanda with a smile. "I noticed it the first day."

Drew's words echoed hollowly in Amanda's head. Kid sister. So that's why Drew was always so attentive!

Amanda had barely absorbed this disappointing piece of information when Drew spoke again, the color rising in his face.

"And Amanda, remember I told you I might have a surprise for you? Well, here she is. Zoe has agreed to marry me," Drew told her. "We're engaged!"

Drew was so pleased with the way that sounded that he bent down to give Zoe a quick kiss. Zoe put her arm through Drew's and moved close to his side.

Amanda smiled mechanically, trying to grasp what Drew had just told her.

Drew is engaged. Drew is getting married. Amanda felt like someone had taken her heart and sliced it open. Her sides ached from the effort of maintaining her composure.

Trying her best to keep a smile on her face, Amanda automatically mouthed the appropriate words of congratulations. Then, pretending to see someone she simply had to speak to, Amanda wobbled off toward the ocean, toward a less crowded part of the beach. Her eyes were streaming with tears.

"Have you spoken to Amanda yet?" Keera asked Hero with concern.

"No, she's been surrounded by all her friends, as usual," Hero replied.

"Have you seen Drew and . . .?" Keera left the end of the sentence off meaningfully.

"Yeah, I've seen him. And I've seen the girlfriend, too," Hero said carefully, not wanting to let on that it mattered.

"Somone should go over and talk to Amanda," Keera suggested softly.

"I was just thinking the same thing," Hero said, looking out in the direction in which he'd seen Amanda walk off.

All at once, the sound system kicked in, and someone blew into the microphone to test it. The electrical equipment pierced the night with a high-pitched squeal, making everyone stop talking and wince.

After Jamar quickly fiddled with the knobs, the noise died down, and he spoke in a clear, ringing voice that echoed all along the beach.

"It's Jammin' time," he said, and, with one crashing note, the music began.

Everyone cheered, since most of them had just seen Jamar's video on KSS. From a collective, swaying press of bodies, the crowd broke down into couples and began to dance.

Except for Hero, who was slowly walking backward out of the undulating path of the dancers.

Except for Keera, who momentarily forgot about Amanda in the shock of hearing Jamar's voice over the microphone, and was now moving toward the bandstand. A surprised smile played around her lips as she moved in time to the music.

Except for Amanda, who was too numb to hear the music or notice the dancing. She was too busy replaying the last five minutes over and over, sitting on one of the uncushioned benches that were scattered along the beach.

The rhythm of the ocean waves banged against her consciousness, overpowering the echoing sounds of Jamar's music. As the unrelenting sound of the waves washed through her, a childish rhyme she'd sung a million times when she was eight or nine years old popped into her head from out of nowhere.

"Drew and Zoe sitting in a tree,

K-I-S-S-I-N-G. First comes love, then comes marriage, then comes Zoe with a baby carriage."

Amanda remembered how she and Samantha used to skip rope to that rhyme, and how Samantha used her own and Tyler's names. Amanda had a vague memory of Tyler singing the song with them before his father pulled him away, telling him he should be playing football, not jumping rope with the girls.

Mr. Scott had sure gotten that wrong. Amanda smiled a little through her tears, remembering Hero's "Flip Side" video.

Amanda sighed as she tilted back her head and wiped away the tears that escaped out of the corners of her eyes and streaked down her cheeks. It had all been so silly and so simple back then.

Gazing up at the first star that was twinkling in the sky, Amanda closed her eyes and made a wish. For just one moment, Amanda longed to go back to "then." "Now" was just too complicated.

Chapter Sixteen

*F*or the better part of half an hour, Samantha Walker had been circling the dancing couples along the beach, looking for Tyler Scott. In her brightly colored halter dress, tightly fitted around the bodice, Samantha was hard to miss. If Tyler had wanted to find her, he wouldn't have had any trouble.

"He told me he'd be here at 8:00," Samantha muttered to herself. "Here it is 8:30, the first of the fireworks is going to go off in half an hour, and if I don't find him soon, I won't have anyone to watch the fireworks with." Samantha pouted, pulling down the corners of her mouth, outlined with drippy red lipstick that matched the flowers on her dress.

Spotting Amanda delicately perched on a bench by the ocean, Samantha pushed her way between the dancing couples to reach her.

"Amanda, hi. What are you doing all the

way over here?" Looking at Amanda's face more closely in the fading light, Samantha added, "Gee, Amanda. You look a little puffy. Do you have a cold or something?"

Without giving Amanda an opportunity to reply, Samantha checked her gold watch and turned to scan the crowd once again, asking with annoyance, "Have you seen Tyler anywhere?"

"Tyler? No, I haven't seen him tonight," Amanda answered faintly.

"Hey, Amanda, that man over there looks just like Drew, the guy from work you're so in love with." Samantha paused as she watched Drew put his arm around Zoe and give her a kiss. "But I guess it couldn't be Drew, 'cause he just kissed this sensational-looking redhead in a very sexy dress."

Amanda fought back tears, determined not to let Samantha see her cry. But Samantha had already lost interest in Amanda. She had spotted Tyler in his navy blue polo shirt and khakis. Waving her arm, she tried to catch his attention.

More than anything, Hero wanted to be the one to comfort Amanda. Just thinking about Amanda in pain stabbed at Hero's heart.

But Hero felt torn. He knew Amanda

190

needed a shoulder to cry on, and he desperately wanted it to be his. But would Amanda let him?

The image of Amanda's violet eyes, crackling with anger during their differences over the past two weeks, flashed in his mind. Then he recalled how their eyes had met yesterday, after the screening of the show. His pulse quickened as he remembered the dazzling smile Amanda had given him.

Determined to follow his heart and somehow win Amanda's love, Hero plunged into the mass of dancing bodies.

Tyler surveyed the wriggling couples on the beach with contempt. After his encounter with Hero, Tyler had lost sight of both him and of Amanda. And when the music started up and everyone began to dance, it became impossible for Tyler to track her down.

Then Tyler's eye caught Hero, hurriedly threading his way toward the ocean, out of the dancers' circle. Looking beyond Hero, Tyler caught sight of Samantha's bright, red-flowered dress, her flailing arm, and, then, beside her . . . Amanda.

Tyler's heart caught as he spotted Amanda. Then he smiled his superior smile.

Amanda was the only thing Tyler wanted that he didn't have, the one thing his father couldn't get for him. That only made Tyler want her all the more. Well, tonight he was going to change all that. Tyler planned to show Amanda how superior he was, in every way, to that Motorcycle Boy, Hero Montoya.

Eyes steadily on Amanda, Tyler strode through the dancers, knocking into people left and right, completely disregarding their outraged calls to watch out. Tyler was going to dance with Amanda before Hero did, even if he had to trample everyone in between to do it.

Tonight was the night. Amanda was going to be his.

Samantha smiled happily as she saw Tyler approaching. "Look, Amanda, here comes Tyler now," Samantha said delightedly. She nervously smoothed her dress down over her hips, wet her lips, and waited expectantly for him to ask her to dance.

Amanda looked around halfheartedly to see where Samantha had seen Tyler. Instead she spotted Hero making his way toward the place where she and Samantha were standing.

192

Without knowing why, Amanda felt her heart lighten. Quickly, she ran her hands through her hair, then rubbed the last vestiges of tears from her cheeks, making them rosier.

"Hey, Samantha. Hey, Amanda. Glad I found you," Hero said as he joined them.

"Hi, Hero," Samantha said, waggling her fingers in his direction. Then she turned back to smile brightly at the approaching Tyler.

"Hi, Hero. It's nice to see you, too," Amanda said quietly, giving him an encouraging smile. He looked like he wanted to say something more, but he was having trouble getting it out.

"Great party, huh?" Hero said finally, awkwardly waving his hand out behind him. Inside, he cringed, wishing he'd been able to think of something a little more original, not to mention more sensitive.

Gazing wistfully past Hero's head, Amanda sighed and echoed his words politely, "Yeah, great party." She was disappointed at his words, but she didn't know why. After all, why should she expect anything from Hero?

Then Tyler strode up. Samantha smiled warmly at him, saying in a kittenish voice, "Oh, Tyler. I've been waiting for you all night."

Tyler ignored Samantha, shooting Hero a glance that made Hero feel like he was walking roadkill.

"Amanda, you look beautiful tonight, more beautiful than I've ever seen you look," Tyler said charmingly. "I've really been missing you this summer," he added, his blue eyes gazing directly into hers.

"Thanks, Tyler," Amanda said, blushing slightly.

Seeing Tyler smoothly move in and take over Amanda's attention, saying all the right things in just the right way, Hero shrank back.

Tyler moved closer to Amanda, placing his hands gently on her shoulders. As if on cue, the music in the background changed suddenly, to something slow and sultry.

"Tell me you've been missing me, too, Amanda," Tyler said softly. "We haven't really seen much of each other since you started working at that television job."

Embarrassed by Tyler's physical closeness, Amanda instinctively fell back a step.

"Dance with me, Amanda, please?" Tyler asked winningly, bringing his face closer to hers.

Amanda hesitated. Looking into Tyler's handsome face, his icy blue eyes, she knew he wanted to kiss her. Amanda could practically feel Tyler's thoughts, knew he wanted to fold her against him and crush his mouth to hers.

For a moment, Amanda considered it. Perhaps letting Tyler take her over would help her forget the pain of seeing Drew and Zoe together.

Hero took another step back. Amanda had already forgotten he was alive. Slowly Hero retreated from the scene, unable to tear his eyes away from the sight of Tyler with his hands on Amanda's shoulders, silhouetted against the darkening night.

Amanda searched for something, some little hint of love in Tyler's eyes. Instead, she saw a look of triumph, as though Tyler had already won her, despite the pleading tone he had affected.

In that moment, Amanda realized that Tyler wanted to own her, like he owned lots of pretty things, not love her. It was love and tenderness, a sympathy of spirit, that Amanda had been hoping to find with Drew. It was clear Tyler wasn't offering that.

Glancing down, Amanda replied gently, "Thanks, Tyler, but I don't really feel like dancing right now."

Immediately, Tyler's look of triumph turned to icy bitterness. The pupils in his blue eyes receded into black dots. Then the music stopped suddenly. There was an awkward silence a mile wide.

Into that silence, Jamar's voice boomed, announcing that the fireworks would start in about fifteen minutes, but that the music would continue until then. The music started up again, and couples slowly drifted down the beach to the water, laying blankets down on the sand so they could watch the fireworks.

Then, as though his conversation with Amanda had never taken place, Tyler turned to Samantha and said, "Come on, let's go brave the wind and waves and watch the fireworks down by the water. We'll keep each other warm."

"Oh Tyler, you're such a romantic," Samantha said, a victorious smile plastered across her face. "See you later, Amanda," Samantha called smugly over her shoulder, as she quickly trailed Tyler away from the crowded shore further down the water line.

Just then, Keera came up behind Amanda. "Boo," Keera said.

Amanda gave a little start.

"I'm sorry, Amanda, I didn't mean to scare you," Keera said apologetically.

"It's all right, Keera," Amanda said. "I'm so glad you're here." Impulsively, Amanda gave her a quick hug. Tyler and Samantha were acting so strangely, but Keera was so normal, Amanda thought. She was grateful that she and Keera had become friends.

"I'm glad I finally found you," Keera said, returning Amanda's hug. "I've been looking for you for ages. Jamar's abandoned me for his music, of course." Keera made a face, but Amanda could tell that she wasn't really mad.

"You two finally worked things out, didn't you?" Amanda asked. "Love's supposed to be like that, isn't it?" she added wistfully.

Keera realized then that Amanda must have already seen Drew with that other woman.

"Are you going to be okay, Amanda . . . about Drew?" Keera asked with gentle concern.

Amanda looked at Keera in surprise. "How did you . . .?"

"I saw Drew when I was looking around for you and Hero—"

"Hero!" Amanda gasped. She just remembered that she and Hero had been talking before all that nonsense with Tyler. Hero must have witnessed it, Amanda realized. Two bright red spots suddenly appeared on her face.

"Where is Hero? I was talking to him before, but then we kind of lost track of each other," Keera said.

"He's here, or, at least, he *was* here. Then Tyler came over, and I guess Hero must have left," Amanda said unhappily. Drawing a shaky breath, she continued, "There's something I have to ask you, Keera. Does everyone know how stupid I've been about Drew?"

Keera gave a tiny nod.

"Does Hero know?" Amanda asked anxiously. Suddenly, she had to know what Hero thought.

Keera hesitated before she answered.

"Keera, it's important. Does Hero know?" Amanda asked again, more urgently.

Keera nodded again. "Hero said he was going to go talk to you, to try to . . ." Keera broke off again, not sure whether or not she should reveal Hero's feelings for Amanda.

"That's why Hero came over." Amanda realized suddenly what it was Hero had been trying to do.

Throwing caution to the wind, Keera took a deep breath and said, "You know, Amanda, I didn't want to say anything about this before, especially with you so wrapped up in Drew and everything, but I think Hero's in love with you. I'm pretty sure he's been crazy about you since that first day at work."

Amanda's face turned completely red. "Oh, I feel like a total idiot," Amanda said, holding her cold hands up to her flushed face. Suddenly, everything clicked into place. No wonder she'd been feeling so funny whenever Hero was around!

"I know how you can feel better," Keera suggested gently.

"How?"

"Find Hero and ask him to watch the fireworks with you," Keera told her.

"Do you think he'll even speak to me?" Amanda asked uncertainly.

Without warning, a whistling filled the air. Streaks of fire shot up into the night sky, and plumes of smoke trailed after them. The rocket flares exploded into gorgeous bursts of light. The fireworks had begun.

Just then Jamar swooped down upon Keera and Amanda, giving them both an exuberant bear hug and carrying them down toward the water.

"So, what did you think of the performance, lovely ladies?" Jamar asked, shouting above the sound of the rockets whistling overhead.

"The band was cool," Amanda told him.

"The music was good. But who said you

could run off and desert me like that?" Keera asked in mock anger.

"I wouldn't desert you, Keera, not ever," Jamar solemnly promised. "Didn't Rogue tell you we were going to play? He told me that while I was setting up the keyboard, he would let you know what was up," Jamar said.

Rogue again! What kind of game was he trying to play? Keera wondered in annoyance. Keera sensed that Rogue was intent upon keeping Jamar and her apart. Well, she wasn't going to let him! Keera decided, turning her face up to the fireworks.

Amanda ducked out from under Jamar's arm and set off along the shoreline. "I'll catch up with you guys later," she called over her shoulder. "There's something I have to do."

Jamar started to call her back. Then Keera whispered in Jamar's ear, and he nodded.

"I think I saw Hero over by Bluff Rock," Jamar shouted after Amanda.

"Thanks," Amanda called back. She headed for Hero, her heart growing happier with each step.

Chapter Seventeen

*T*yler spotted Amanda walking toward the looming Bluff Rock. Mumbling something about the call of nature, Tyler excused himself and told Samantha he'd be back in a while with a surprise.

"Oooh, Tyler, I just love surprises," Samantha oozed, looking up at Tyler coyly. But she needn't have bothered, Tyler was already gone.

Doubling behind the couples dotting the shoreline, Tyler walked parallel to Amanda long enough to figure out where she was headed. It wasn't hard to figure out, once he saw Hero standing alone beneath the overhang of Bluff Rock.

Perfect, Tyler thought grimly. It's time to take care of Hero Montoya once and for all. Tyler headed toward the parking lot, anxious to exhibit his latest toy—his brand new Fatboy Softail Harley motorcycle.

Donning his black visored helmet, Tyler gunned the engine and roared off, taking the back path to the top of Bluff Rock. He had a surprise for Hero—and Amanda, too.

Hero stood, facing the sea, enjoying the cold, stinging spray that danced over his face. He was intent upon watching the waves crash against the supporting boulders, instead of looking up to the sky, like everyone else, to watch the fireworks.

Then he sensed a presence moving toward him.

A single barefoot figure stood in the moonlight, the bottom edge of her dress clinging to her legs while her hair whipped wildly around her head. It seemed as though a mermaid had emerged from the crashing surf, surrounded by a fine mist of ocean spray that hovered over the waves as they broke on the sand.

Hero blinked hard. His eyes must be playing tricks on him. For a second, it looked like Amanda was standing in the water, looking at him, waiting. His imagination was running wild tonight, he told himself, turning his face back to the sea. He'd been wishing that Amanda were here with him, and, suddenly, Amanda magically appeared.

If only life was really like that. If only you could wish something hard enough—

on a star, or whatever they used in those syrupy fairy tales his mother used to tell him—and the wish could come true.

It was all a crock, Hero thought unhappily. What the fairy tales never told you was that all wishing did was make the hurt worse.

The sky exploded in a rainbow of colors, illuminating Amanda's ivory-colored dress and windblown hair. Amanda's eyes glowed brightly, shining like mirrors as they reflected the light.

Hero looked over again. This time, his eyes opened wide. "Amanda?" Hero said in a disbelieving whisper, raking his hair back over his head.

The lights in the sky faded out then, and a cloud passed in front of the moon, plunging the ocean and sky into a quiet, velvety darkness.

"Amanda?" Hero called again, louder this time.

Amanda jumped when Hero called her name. As if waking from a dream, Amanda began to move slowly, uncertainly, toward Hero.

"Hero!" Amanda called in a small voice that could barely be heard against the waves.

Amanda stood before Hero then. Her

hair was wild, released to the wind. Her dress was damp, her feet were crusted with wet sand. She had never looked more beautiful to Hero.

Amanda stared hard into Hero's perfect face, searching for the signs of anger or hatred that she was so afraid would be there. She looked without flinching into his shining eyes, and they told her everything.

"Hero, I . . . " Amanda began, moving closer to him.

At the same time, Hero started to say, "Amanda, what . . ."

But before either of them could complete their thoughts, the sound of a powerful engine roared from above Bluff Rock.

"Who the . . .?" Hero asked, stepping out from under the overhang. He craned his neck upward, protectively holding Amanda behind him.

"It's showdown time, Motorcycle Boy," Tyler shouted over the waves, raising his visor so that Hero could see and hear him.

Then Tyler flipped down his visor, gunned the engine, and raced down the narrow footpath to the beach. He pointed his motorcycle directly toward Hero.

Pushing Amanda out of harm's way, Hero stood his ground as Tyler roared dead-on toward him. Amanda stood, frozen, unable to believe what she was seeing.

Tyler swerved at the last moment, digging his wheels hard into the ground and spraying Hero and Amanda with sand. He came to a stop less than a foot away from Hero.

Hero hadn't flinched. "Kind of a long way from the benches on the football field, isn't it?" he said calmly.

Lifting his visor, Tyler said, "I thought we'd play your kind of game tonight, Motorcycle Boy. I've been saving this little surprise for a special occasion, and tonight's the night! Just you and me, down Cliff Point Road. Your wheels against mine. And this time, there'll be no cameras or buddies to hide behind."

"Don't do it, Hero," Amanda said. "It's too dangerous. Cliff Point Road isn't wide enough for two motorcycles." She remembered how many bad accidents had happened on Cliff Point Road in the past.

"Meet me at the top in twenty minutes. Unless, of course, you're afraid," Tyler said mockingly.

Hero's body tensed again, like a tiger waiting to pounce. His pulse was racing, the blood throbbing against his skull.

Hero knew that he and Tyler had been

destined for this since they'd met on the football field. If a showdown is what he wants, then a showdown is what he'll get, Hero swore to himself through clenched teeth.

"I'll see you there, rich boy." Hero spit out the words.

"Agreed," Tyler said coldly. Then he looked at Amanda.

"Let's make it really interesting. Amanda rides with the winner. What do you say?" Tyler challenged. "That seems only fair. Two jousting knights, and the winner gets the girl!"

Thrusting her chin out, Amanda glared at Tyler. "I'm not something you can win, Tyler," she said angrily. "And you know that Cliff Point Road is too dangerous. You could both be killed."

Tyler just laughed. Then he flipped his visor back down, gunned the engine once more, and rode off, spraying sand behind him as he raced down the beach.

"Hero, please don't do this. Tyler's just jealous. But you don't have to do this, not for me," Amanda pleaded with Hero, grabbing his hand.

At the touch of her hand, Hero stopped dead in the sand. For so long he'd been dreaming of Amanda's touch, thinking about how her creamy skin would feel against his. And now, everything was all wrong. Her hand felt cold and clammy against his own damp skin.

Gently extracting his hand from hers, Hero turned and held her bare arms in his hands.

Amanda shivered at the touch of Hero's skin against hers. His roughened fingers pressed lightly against her arms, momentarily caressing her before letting her go.

"Amanda," Hero began, the name falling softly from his lips, as if he could hardly believe he had the right to say it. "I can't explain. But I do have to do this—for me. Before I—I mean, before we—can do anything else."

"But I never got the chance to tell you . . ." Amanda began.

Hero put his finger gently to her soft lips. "Not now, Amanda. Not yet. When this is over . . ." Hero's voice trailed off, and he walked quickly away, his heart breaking. He knew there was no telling if he would be back, or if Amanda would be waiting for him.

Standing in the sand, watching Hero leave her, Amanda felt chilled to the bone. She was sure she'd never be warm again.

"Amanda, what's up? Where's Hero

going?" Keera came running over, full of questions.

"Where's Jamar?" Amanda asked anxiously.

"Oh, his friend Rogue came over and asked him to play one last set before the final fireworks," Keera said. She was annoyed, remembering how she had been blissfully leaning against Jamar's strong arm, watching the fireworks, when Rogue had jostled them apart and teased Jamar into going back for another set. "I saw you standing here, and I thought you might want someone to talk to—"

"We need to find Jamar," Amanda broke in urgently. She remembered how Jamar had stopped Hero from slugging it out with Tyler on the football field. Maybe Jamar could do something about this suicidal motorcycle race.

"How come?" Keera asked, sensing serious trouble.

"I'll explain on the way," Amanda told her. "We haven't got much time." Then she took off toward the bandstand with Keera close on her heels.

Chapter Eighteen

*E*ven before Amanda and Keera had finished explaining Tyler's challenge to Hero, Jamar had jumped down off the bandstand, leaving his buddies to carry on without him.

Rogue gave Keera an unhappy stare, which she chose to ignore. But as she jogged along side Jamar and Amanda, Keera made a mental note to talk about Rogue with Jamar later.

Word of the impending showdown had spread quickly, and a crowd had gathered at the dirt road where Cliff Point Road abruptly ended. Amanda, Keera, and Jamar pushed their way to the front. But it was crystal clear that they were already too late to prevent the race.

"There they are," Jamar said, pointing helplessly to the top of Cliff Point.

Both motorcycles were in position. Both riders had their helmets on, heads down, and were revving their engines, louder and louder.

"Oh, no," Amanda groaned. There was no way of stopping Tyler and Hero now. All they could do was watch and wait.

As if in a dream, Hero had walked away from Amanda, heading unswervingly toward his classic '66 cycle. Time stood still. All the other night noises—couples laughing, echoing strains of music, occasional firecrackers—fell away into a great yawning silence.

Hero felt as though he were walking in slow motion underwater. He had left Amanda reluctantly, moving inexorably toward the darkness that awaited him. Two voices echoed over and over in Hero's head. He heard Amanda call his name as if from some faraway place. Then Tyler's taunting voice echoed louder and louder through Hero's skull, "Afraid, afraid, afraid?"

Hero swung onto his Harley. He was glad that he'd spent the day working on the amplified engine. Otherwise, this race would be no contest.

Pulling on his white-topped helmet, Hero revved the souped-up engine and took off. Driving blindly past the partygoers at the beach, Hero began his ascent up the path that led from the beach to the top of Cliff Point.

Hero didn't notice the crowd that had gathered at the end of Cliff Point Road. All he saw was Tyler mounted on his powerful new Harley, the polished chrome glinting in the moonlight, waiting for Hero in the darkness.

Hero swung his motorcycle parallel to Tyler's. He stared down the steep, winding pathway, which was never intended to accommodate two vehicles. Hero could smell the sea and hear the surf several hundred feet beneath the shore side of the road.

"When the firecrackers go off," Tyler shouted over the wind and the surf, "that's the signal." He revved his engine loudly.

Hero revved his engine in response, without looking at Tyler. Squeezing his legs tighter around the body of the cycle, Hero waited for the race to start.

From where he sat, he could almost see Amanda waiting for him at the bottom of the road. Closing his eyes, Hero imagined that he was standing before her, as he had on the beach. Her eyes filled with love as his lips tenderly covered hers.

That's how this night should have gone, Hero told himself, blinking back to the real world.

Suddenly, the sharp *rat-a-tat-tat* of the

firecrackers pierced the night. The sky exploded into a thousand tiny red, white, and blue flames of light, illuminating the two rivals hovering precariously on the narrow edge of Cliff Point.

As if shot out of the same cannon, both motorcycles catapulted down the steep, winding road, as flickering lights continued to bombard the sky. But no one watched the fireworks at all. No one could tear their eyes away from the two cyclists as they careened along Cliff Point Road.

Hero and Tyler raced nose to nose for as long as the road permitted. As the road narrowed, Tyler turned his cycle ever so slightly toward Hero's front wheel, intending to nudge him off the edge. But Hero, the more experienced driver of the two, turned his bike sharply out of Tyler's way.

Amanda's heart leaped into her mouth and her breathing stopped. It looked like Hero was going to go right over the cliff.

Then Hero turned his wheel sharply back, flooring the cycle to jump ahead of Tyler. Hero now owned the slope side of the path, while Tyler was forced to ride on the drop-dead overhang above the beach.

Hero smiled grimly, not permitting himself to think that the race was won. He had to keep his inside edge, keep con-centrating, taking one turn at a time, then the next one, and the next. A moment's hesitation and Tyler would be on him. There was no doubt in either one's mind that this was a fight to the finish.

Quickly recovering from Hero's deft maneuver, Tyler pulled out the throttle of his own powerful machine and recklessly charged along the outside edge. He was determined to eliminate Hero from the race once and for all.

Both riders swept along the path, with Hero slightly in the lead. Engines roared and tires squealed at every turn as the road swerved down the cliff.

Tyler had almost caught up to Hero, but, with Hero hugging the inside edge of the road, Tyler was unable to pass him. Frustrated by Hero's lead, Tyler pointed his cycle directly at Hero's, intending to knock him off the road and send him tumbling down the slope.

Hero's cycle roared off the path, almost out of control. He slowed down, struggling to navigate the overgrown, needle-sharp brush that grew along the slope.

The crowd held its breath, waiting to see whether or not Hero would be able to regain control and get back in the race.

Amanda could barely watch. To her, it all seemed hopeless.

Laughing at Hero's difficulty, Tyler pulled up farther along the road, just before the narrowest, sharpest turn, where both the slope edge and the cliff side were a sheer hundred-foot drop. He intended to watch every detail of Hero's defeat.

But Hero was not defeated. Hanging desperately onto his bike, he managed to turn it back on the path.

Tyler's laughter died when he realized Hero was back in the race. In his hurry to open the throttle, Tyler's foot slipped off the pedal. The cycle lurched forward. Tyler was barely able to regain control before Hero bore down on him—fast.

It was clear that both rivals were going to take the last and worst hairpin turn of all at exactly the same time. There was no way that two riders could take that turn together and live.

"Hero," Amanda whispered, her lips dry, fear tasting bitter in her mouth.

Hero realized that, in order to make the final turn, he would have to push Tyler over the edge. For a moment, he envisioned Tyler and his cycle flipping off the cliff. He could almost hear the sickening crunch of Tyler's cycle and his body against the sharp rocks below.

At the same time, Hero imagined Amanda's face, filled with horror at the sight of Tyler, her friend, lying crumpled and broken against the rocks. She would turn against Hero in anger for what he had done.

A moment before impact, Hero forced his bike away from Tyler's. He roared down the precarious slope, permitting Tyler to take the turn on his own. Tyler raced triumphantly down the incline to the finish line where everyone was waiting.

But no one greeted him. All eyes were on Hero as he wrestled with his bike, unwilling to let it go, but unable to control it down the slope.

Amidst the flickering fireworks that lent an unreal quality to the entire scene, Hero dropped, free falling in slow motion. The ground came up suddenly beneath him.

His beloved motorcycle bounced its way down the slope, narrowly missing Hero as he rolled over and over and over. The tumbleweed scratched at his hands as he tried to cling to it and tore at his jeans as his legs caught on the brush.

Somewhere between the tumbleweed and the rocks, Hero lost consciousness. He came to rest at the bottom of the slope, his body limp.

Chapter Nineteen

*F*or a moment, nobody moved.

Then, with a sharp cry, Amanda started toward Hero's still form.

Tyler was furious that no one had congratulated him on winning the race. He threw down his motorcycle and caught up to Amanda, holding her back from Hero's motionless body.

"Forget about him, Amanda. Let someone else clean up after that loser," Tyler said scornfully.

"Let go of me, Tyler. You're the one who's the loser, not Hero," Amanda said, struggling fiercely out of Tyler's grasp.

"Oh, come on, Amanda. You're not going to let this new guy come between us and all the years we've been friends, are you?"

"At this moment, you don't look like any friend of mine," Amanda said, breaking free of Tyler's grasp.

Tyler was about to go after Amanda, but Jamar deftly stepped in front of him. In disgust, Tyler stalked off.

Amanda knelt beside Hero's motionless form. The bottom of her ivory lace dress dragged in the dirt, but it didn't matter. Nothing mattered but Hero.

Amanda looked over the length of Hero's still, hard body. She was afraid to touch him, afraid to hurt him.

Gently, Amanda removed his white helmet, now all dented and scratched, and placed it behind her. Amanda gasped when she saw blood dripping from a cut on Hero's chin, oozing down his neck, trickling onto the edge of his black shirt.

"Hero, it's Amanda," she whispered, her lips close to his ear.

Hero groaned and shifted slightly.

Amanda's heart started to beat again. Hero was alive! He could move!

"Hero, can you hear me?" Amanda whispered again. She moved even closer to Hero, until she was cradling his head on her lap. Gently she stroked Hero's soft brown hair, now matted to his forehead with sweat.

At Amanda's tender touch, Hero's eyes fluttered open and he tried to sit up. For a moment, everything was blurry. Dark images hovered above him.

All of a sudden, the clouds vanished,

and the full moon shone brightly down on Hero and Amanda. Squinting from the light, Hero closed his eyes and sank back down.

Amanda leaned down, barely touching Hero's lips with her own. Her long silky hair fell over her face, brushing against Hero's cheeks.

"Hero, it's Amanda," she whispered again. Tears escaped from the corners of her eyes, trickling slowly down her cheeks. If only Hero would answer her, so she would know that he was going to be okay!

At that moment, Hero opened his eyes. "Hey, Amanda," he said weakly. He lifted his hand, fingering a golden lock of hair and gently hooking it behind Amanda's ear, so that he could see all of her beautiful face. He was surprised at her tears.

"Tears for me, Amanda?" Hero asked, pressing his thumbs lightly onto the wetness that stained her cheeks and wiping it from her skin.

Amanda nodded, unable to speak.

Hero struggled to his feet, wincing with pain. Amanda reached to hold him up.

"Where does it hurt? I mean where does it hurt most?" Amanda asked with concern.

Hero thought for a moment. Then he lightly tapped his lips.

"Are you sure?" Amanda asked, incredulous. She hadn't noticed any bruises around his mouth.

With an impish grin, Hero looked directly into Amanda's luminous violet eyes and said, "I was hoping you'd want to make it all better."

Amanda realized then that Hero was going to be just fine. Looking deeply into his brown eyes, Amanda replied simply, "I'd love to."

Hero drew Amanda to him, pressing her tenderly against his body. She could feel the tautness of his stomach, the hardness of his chest. Amanda tilted her head, eyes closed, waiting for him to lower his mouth to hers.

Hero paused for a moment. "Amanda," he whispered. He had to make sure this was real, that he wasn't dead or dreaming.

"I love you, Amanda," Hero said solemnly.

"I love you, Hero," Amanda whispered solemnly back.

Slowly, Hero brought his face down to hers. Their lips touched, softly at first. Then their mouths pressed hard against each other.

With one swift movement, Hero pulled Amanda even closer. He kissed her eyes, her nose, the smooth, creamy skin of her face, tasting of salty tears. Then, once again, he found her mouth hungrily with his lips.

Amanda clung to Hero. She felt as though she were falling through a long, empty space—and the only thing that connected her to solid ground was Hero.

A low whistle sounded above them. Once again, the air was filled with hurling flares—purple, orange, blue, green—all seeking the highest point of the night sky and giving the beach the appearance of day.

Everyone could see that Hero was obviously all right. Some of the crowd wandered off, back to the remnants of the party. Others started to cheer—for Hero, for the fireworks, for sheer relief at the break in the tension.

But neither Hero nor Amanda noticed a thing.

As the last of the Independence Day flares died out in the sky, Hero and Amanda turned away from the crowd.

Arm in arm, Keera and Jamar watched them walk off together. With Hero's arm securely draped over Amanda's shoulder and her arm encircling Hero's waist, they headed back toward Bluff Rock—where their evening had almost begun—to pick up where they had left off, before Tyler, before the race.

It was time to make this a private celebration. Their show was a success. The summer ahead promised to be long and happy. Nothing and nobody else mattered at all.